What if she physically could not bring the person responsible for Kit's death to justice?

Latham had leaned back into his chair, his gaze thoughtful, arms folded across his chest. His eyes seemed to look right through her, focused on an unseen target. Heather recognized the look on his face. He was solving a case deep in the recesses of his mind.

And with a bum leg and strict orders to steer clear of the investigation, she'd never crack the case before he did. At least with him, she'd have access to all of his connections, research and mobility.

Suddenly she wanted to tell Latham everything she knew. Tell him about the crash and Kit's worries. Tell him that she knew this wasn't an accident. But what if he wasn't willing to help her? She had to get his word, had to get him to agree.

Swallowing thickly, she closed her eyes for a moment. "There's more," she said.

Books by Liz Johnson

Love Inspired Suspense

The Kidnapping of Kenzie Thorn
Vanishing Act
Code of Justice

LIZ JOHNSON

After graduating from Northern Arizona University in Flagstaff with a degree in public relations, Liz Johnson set out to work in the Christian publishing industry, which was her lifelong dream. In 2006 she got her wish when she accepted a publicity position with a major trade book publisher. While working as a publicist in the industry, she decided to pursue her other dream—becoming an author. Along the way to having her novels published, she wrote articles for several magazines and worked as a freelance editorial consultant.

Liz makes her home in Nashville, Tennessee, where she enjoys theater, exploring her new home and making frequent trips to Arizona to dote on her nephew and three nieces. She loves stories of true love with happy endings.

CODE OF JUSTICE

Liz Johnson

Steeple
Hill®

Published by Steeple Hill Books™

STEEPLE HILL BOOKS

Steeple
Hill®

Recycling programs
for this product may
not exist in your area.

ISBN-13: 978-0-373-44434-2

CODE OF JUSTICE

He has showed you, O man, what is good.
And what does the Lord require of you?
To act justly and to love mercy
and to walk humbly with your God.
—*Micah* 6:8

For my sisters.

Hannah, I could not have written a book about
sisters without knowing the magnitude
of that bond firsthand. Here's to another thirty years
of laughter, tears and pedicures.

Beth, I'm so glad you chose to become
part of our family. When you married Micah,
I truly gained another sister.

Your sacrifices are countless.
Your examples are inspiring.
Your friendships are matchless.
Thank you.

PROLOGUE

"Ladies, you better make sure you're buckled up. Now!" the pilot said. The sightseeing helicopter gave a vicious lurch and started losing altitude. "The cyclic isn't responding! We're going down!"

Heather Sloan jostled the belt around her waist until it was secure, then grabbed across the seat for the hand of her sister Kit, the only other passenger.

Kit's green eyes eclipsed the rest of her thin face, which was even more pale than usual. Her grip was devastating, and Heather quickly lost feeling in three fingers. Their eyes remained locked as the pilot growled frantically to himself.

"What's happening?" Kit's words were so soft that Heather couldn't even hear her through the headset and had to read her lips.

"I don't know," she said with a shake of her head. She tried to squeeze the other woman's hand, but the aircraft dropped then bounced as if attached to a rubber band as the engine wheezed and the rotor went silent. Stomach lodged firmly in her throat, Heather blinked at the tears that formed in the corner of her eyes. Tears that mirrored her sister's. As an FBI agent, Heather was used to danger. But when she was on a case, she knew to be prepared for what she might face. She wasn't prepared for this. How had a simple day trip with her sister gone so wrong so fast?

"Hold on! Tight!" growled Jack DeWitt, the grizzly man in front of them, as he madly punched red, flashing buttons on the dashboard. "I've lost all control! Something's wrong with the back rotor!"

Out of the corner of her eye, Heather spied the strangely slanted horizon on the other side of the wide window. But it wasn't the horizon that was off. It was the angle of the helicopter as they plunged toward the forest below.

Wrestling to maintain control, Jack grunted, sparing a glance over his shoulder to confirm that his only two passengers were belted in. He offered them a curt nod before returning to the problem at hand. Grabbing the small black radio at the corner of his mouth, he yelled something that was lost behind the rushing in Heather's ears.

"It's going to be okay," she whispered, more to herself than Kit. Then for all of them, she sent up a quick prayer for safety. "Lord, please let us walk away from this."

The seats began shaking with the force of Jack trying to keep the aircraft aloft. It felt as if the doors were going to rip off and the paneling would simply disintegrate.

"Heather, I love you."

"I love you, too, Kit." Her little sister's dark hair and green eyes were the opposite of her own fair complexion, but their features were the same, and for an instant Heather couldn't help but wonder if her own face reflected the same terror.

"I meant to tell you—" The floor panels rattled, drowning out Kit's words. "Heather," she tried again, her white hands squeezing even tighter. "I needed to tell you—"

And then there was nothing but the crashing of trees crunching and scrape of wood against metal—worse than fingernails on a chalkboard.

Heather's head jerked to the side, slamming against the window, making her bite her tongue, and she cried out.

The helicopter rolled to the right, and then the left, tossing the two helpless passengers at its whim. Light seemed to come and go as brush covered the windows, disappearing as quickly as it arrived.

Heather had no time to think, no time to react. She could only watch as the lightweight aircraft shuddered and the door farthest away from her peeled away. Tree limbs battered Kit, and no matter how hard she tugged, Heather couldn't get her sister away from the brutal abuse.

It seemed to last for hours.

It was over in a flash.

Finally, the plane came to rest on the ground. From the cockpit, Jack had gone silent. Beside Heather, so had Kit. Panic started to build. Fighting the pain growing behind her temple from where she'd hit her head, Heather scrambled to reach Kit's side. Pain shot through her left leg and right shoulder, from which hung her useless arm.

Ignoring it all, she reached for her sister, brushing long brown strands from her nicked and bruised face. A pool of blood on Kit's left thigh grew rapidly.

"Kit? Kit, can you hear me?"

Green eyes, filled with pain, opened to half-mast. "I meant to tell you…"

"Shh. It's okay. Help will be here soon. It's okay."

"Heather. Please. Drugs."

"I don't have anything for you. I don't have anything for the pain." Kit's grip relaxed slightly, and Heather clung to her hand, holding it to her chest. "Please. Hang on."

"Follow..."

"Shh." A teardrop splashed on their hands, but it was several moments before Heather realized that it was her own.

Kit closed her eyes, swallowed and tried again. "Follow the drugs," she breathed.

Heather couldn't let go, even though she knew her sister had. She clung to Kit's hand as darkness consumed her.

ONE

Heather's mind had been mostly foggy with only a brief respite for days. The medication the doctor had given her made it hard to remember how many days had passed or who had been to visit her since she first arrived at the hospital. Had it been three days? Maybe four?

She couldn't be sure when she had last been awake, but as the haze rolled away this time, her brain felt less fuzzy, and she was able to concentrate on the sound of footsteps on tile. Then a gentle touch on her arms and leg. Then searing pain in her left leg. She could manage only a whimper. Then there was a prick on the back of her hand and a voice she didn't recognize. "She pulled it out again."

None of the past days made any sense, no matter how hard she tried to pull them all into focus. Her brain felt like mush, her memory hibernating.

Soon the pain ebbed, and she sighed, sinking a little deeper into the pillow beneath her head. Light flashed before her closed eyes, and she tried to open them, but they refused to respond.

After several minutes another set of footsteps entered the room, this one lighter and punctuated by the staccato taps of high heels. The steps quick and purposeful. A gentle voice said, "How's she doing?"

She knew that voice.

"No—" Her voice cracked, but she tried again. "Nora?" The sound was barely audible, but immediately a warm hand slid into hers.

"Heather. I'm here."

Slowly, her mind started to clear through the haze of the drugs they'd given her. Nora. Nora James. Who was engaged to Nate Andersen, her supervisor at the Bureau.

"Do you want some water?"

She nodded, but was met with resistance under her chin. The neck brace. The leg brace. They had repaired her torn ACL, which had been shredded in the crash.

The crash.

It all hit at once and tears leaked between her closed eyelids, running down the sides of her face. A smooth knuckle slid along her temples, wiping the drops away. Then a plastic straw pushed against her lips. She drank several long sips before Nora pulled it away.

Fighting the pain that wanted to keep her eyes closed and brain turned off, she opened them a crack. Nora's kind features and long blond hair were blurry but unmistakable.

"How are you doing, sweetie?" She squeezed Heather's hand. "Do you need anything else?"

Heather opened her mouth, but couldn't push another word past her throat. Was Nate here, too? She didn't want him to see her like this. Please say he hadn't already been to visit.

And then the footfalls that had walked past her office for nearly three years entered her hospital room. "Sorry I'm late, ladies." Nate stepped up to the bed, leaning over just enough so she could see his ever-present five o'clock shadow, which looked longer than usual. He rubbed it with one palm as he pulled up a chair closer to her bed. "Just had another phone call with Mitch. He's worried about you, kid. Everyone at the office is."

"I'm fine," Heather managed just before another wave of pain from her shoulder stole her breath.

Nate wrapped his arm around Nora's waist but seemed to lean in closer to Heather, even if she could barely see him out of the corner of her eye. "It's good to see you. You look good."

Liar.

She looked awful, and she didn't even need a mirror to know it.

And she looked weak. She felt weak. She just didn't want Nate to see her in this state. Would he think she couldn't handle an assignment after seeing her like this?

"Nate." She sighed, finally offering him half of a smile. "You're a good boss, but I wish you wouldn't have come."

He chuckled. "You're on a lot of medication. You'll think otherwise when you're back to normal." Picking and choosing what he heard had always been his way with her.

She managed a tiny shake of her head, despite the neck brace and heavy fog threatening to roll back in. She blinked again, trying desperately to make her mind return to its normal speed.

"We were here yesterday with Mitch and Myles and Kenzie, too. You just didn't have the decency to wake up to greet us."

She had woken up yesterday, though not while her friends or family were there. She wished her timing had been better. Maybe it wouldn't have hurt so much if she'd been told by her parents or friends that she was the crash's only survivor—that Kit was dead.

Still she offered the obligatory apology that she knew Nate was waiting for. "Sorry."

He chuckled again and squeezed her hand briefly before letting it go.

"The nurse said you were talking about your gun in your sleep last night," Nora said. "I think you were looking for it and pulled out your IV instead."

Nate's shoulders jostled as a broad smile spread across his face. Since he'd returned from his last assignment where he met Nora, he'd been smiling and laughing a lot more than usual. "I guess I shouldn't have expected anything else from you. But don't worry about it. I'll keep it safe until you're released."

Heather scowled, her hand searching for the cool handle of her Glock out of pure habit. She pleaded with her eyes for him to give her back her gun, but Nate shook his head. "Nope. You're on way too much medication, not to mention the amount of oxygen just sitting next to your bed. When they let you out of here, you'll get it back." He smirked at the glare she shot his way.

She swallowed again, forcing her vocal cords to recall their job. "How did you get it?"

"Your mom gave it to me. I guess the hospital had it with your clothes and other personal affects." He tugged Nora a little closer and whispered in a mock-conspiratorial tone, "Apparently she had it with her in the helicopter. Because, you know, when I go on a strictly sightseeing tour of Mount Saint Helens and Mount Hood, I always bring my weapon with me."

Nora shoved her fiancé's shoulder. "Give Heather a break."

Heather shrugged, then cringed as pain shot through her shoulder. Twisting as much as her multiple braces and injuries allowed, she turned toward Nate. "So where are my parents? Does the hospital only allow two visitors at a time?"

He looked away then brought his steel blue eyes back to meet hers, all teasing aside. "Listen, Heather, I'm sorry." He swallowed thickly, and her stomach turned with a sudden knowledge.

"Kit's funeral?"

"It was this morning. Nora and I skipped the graveside service. Your mom wanted someone here when you woke up." He studied the spot on the floor between his shoes, and she realized that he was dressed in his best black Hugo Boss. They'd worked together for almost three years, and she could count on one hand the number of times she'd seen him wearing the slick suit.

When he brought his gaze back up to meet hers, all she could see was the pain there—all traces of humor gone. He just shook his head. "I'm sorry you couldn't be there. Your parents wanted to wait, but the doctors don't know how long you're going to be in here. And your dad's unit was called back overseas. He ships out right away, so one or the other of you would have had to miss it. And the funeral home couldn't wait indefinitely, so the director suggested just going ahead with the service."

Through the fierce ache in her shoulder, Heather lifted her hand to her eyes, brushing away two unruly tears.

She'd missed her chance to say goodbye to her little sister. And she didn't have any idea why any of this had happened. Why their helicopter had gone down. What

Kit had meant about following the drugs. None of it made sense.

Yet.

But she would figure it out. Kit was far too special to just let go without a reason.

Reining in her emotions, Heather cleared her throat. "I'll bet my parents told you not to tell me all of that."

"They said they weren't sure you could handle it just yet. I knew otherwise."

"Thank you, Nate. It's better to know. Right?"

"Right."

A yawn caught Heather off guard and made her two friends smile.

"We better get going and let you get some rest. We'll see you tomorrow," Nate said before squeezing Heather's hand and standing at the same time as Nora. Hand in hand they took a step toward the door before Nate suddenly stopped.

"Heather, I need you to promise me something," he said over his shoulder.

"What?" The word was more of a croak than anything else, but he seemed to understand.

"It's going to take you a while to recoup. Give it some time." His brow furrowed, his mouth turning stern. "Don't try to push yourself too hard."

After a long pause, she conceded. "I won't."

He nodded and gave her a knowing look. "And let the police do their job. Stay out of this investigation."

Nate's face softened.

She didn't respond, and he took a firm step toward her, his face a concoction of sharp angles. "I'm not kidding, Sloan." He didn't usually call her by her last name unless he was tired or she was being obstinate. "I need you to focus on getting better. Nothing else. You won't get involved in this case beyond answering whatever questions the investigator has. That's a direct order. Understood?"

She had no other choice but to agree. "Yes."

"Have the nurse call me if you need anything," Nora called from the doorway just before they disappeared. "See you tomorrow."

The way Nate had rested his hand on Nora's back mirrored the familiar actions of Clay Kramer, Kit's fiancé. Except now he wasn't engaged to her anymore. Because she was—

Heather closed her eyes, willing the image of Clay and Kit laughing together the night before the crash to vanish. It faded slightly, leaving only an imagined likeness of the pain Clay was enduring, his handsome face twisted in agony. How could he survive with the love of his life gone? How could *she* ever think of having a happy life with her sister gone?

Beyond questions of her own happiness lay more sinister inquiries that were painful just to ponder. Had someone really wanted to hurt Kit? Why would they want to kill someone everyone loved? Was it possible that Heather's own life could be in jeopardy, too?

These questions haunted her as she fell into a fitful sleep.

Heather heard the rattle and click of the turning door handle before she was consciously awake. Her brain still foggy from sleep and the pain medication, she struggled to open her eyes, wondering if she was having another visitor. Her parents had been by earlier, but she'd insisted they go back to the hotel. She could see how drained they were after the funeral.

At the same moment that the door opened, her eyelids raised enough that she could see through her lashes.

A short, round man ducked into the room, looking over his shoulder as though confirming that he wasn't being followed, before silently closing the door behind him. When he turned to face her, she could make out only his ratty, gray jacket and violently shaking hands. She'd never seen anyone's hands shaking that badly—except drug addicts going through withdrawal.

But what was an addict doing in her hospital room?

He spun around slowly before shuffling toward her bed. She flexed her hand, feeling around for her gun. Which Nate still had. Maybe she could reach the call button on the side of the bed without tipping him off that she was alert—if somewhat groggy. Before scaring him off, she needed to know what he wanted.

A wave of body odor nearly sent her to the floor gagging, and she quickly adjusted to breathing through her mouth.

"Put the tube in the line," the man mumbled. "Put the tube in the line. Then get the fix."

What tube? What line?

The fix was easy enough to understand.

Suddenly he grabbed the IV line attached to the back of her hand, almost tugging it out. She forced her eyes to open all the way, looking into the face of a man with glassy eyes, long white hair and several days of patchy beard growth.

"What are you doing?" she asked, carefully keeping her tone soft, if scratchy.

He didn't look at her, just continuing his chant. "Need to put the tube in the line. Then I get a fix."

"What are you doing?" she asked again, putting more force behind her words as she reached for the call button, praying it would bring help right away. Her words made him glance at her, but it didn't make him pause, as he pulled a small medical vial from his pocket and tried to connect it to her IV. "Stop! Don't do that!"

Even with the tremors in his hands, he moved quickly, slipping the vial into place to feed whatever was in it into the line. She tried to roll to the side to stop him, but the sudden burning in the back of her hand was excruciating.

The man shuffled a step toward the door, as she clawed at her hand, trying to pull the tubing out.

"What is this?" she cried as the fire raced up her arm.

It took her another moment to realize that the blood-curdling scream filling the room came from her own throat.

TWO

Even after Jeremy Latham flashed his Sheriff's Deputy badge at the pretty blonde nurse at the station next to the elevator, she wouldn't tell him the exact condition of the survivor of the helicopter crash that had claimed two lives. Something about confidential patient records. No matter. If she was conscious, he would get Heather Sloan's statement and piece together the events leading up to the crash. But as he approached the door he'd been directed to, a scream sent him running toward the very room the nurse had indicated. As he neared it, a woman shouted again.

Hoping the door was unlocked, he crashed into the solid wood. It flew open as he twisted the handle, sending him to his knees on the slick floor.

A pair of very old shoes and an unpleasant odor shuffled past him as he scrambled to his feet. He caught only a glimpse of the back of the man's head before screams from the bed grabbed his attention.

"Get it out. Get it out! It burns!"

The cries from the woman on the bed made it clear what took priority. She needed help. *Now.* Jeremy ignored the other man as he scrambled to her side.

Putting one hand on her forearm, Jeremy said, "Where does it burn?"

"Right arm," she managed between gritted teeth, her eyes rolling back in her head.

This was no time to pretend he had the kind of medical training needed to help. He pounded the call button over and over, following it up with shouts of his own. "Nurse! Nurse! I need help in 411!"

The young woman screamed when he picked up her arm, but he had to get a closer look at the crimson stripes making their way toward her elbow. She must have pulled the dangling tube from the back of her hand, but the redness definitely started beneath the tape still holding an IV needle in place.

The red lines were nearly to the crook in her arm when he realized that he had to stop whatever was causing them from getting any farther. Yanking the IV cord from its bag he wrapped it around her biceps and jerked it into a crude knot. The slick plastic didn't want to stay in place, so he held it there, calling again for help. "Nurse!"

The woman whimpered, and he put his hand back on her forehead.

"It's going to be okay. You're all right."

Just then, the same blonde nurse who had told him Heather was in room 411 entered at a run, and her presence made Jeremy breathe a little easier, despite her curt tone. "What happened in here?"

"I don't know. I was in the hallway, and I heard someone screaming. There was another man in here. I think he put something in her IV. She said that it was burning her. I tried to stop it from going any farther up her arm." He raised his hands to show her the makeshift tourniquet.

The patient groaned, her eyes still clamped shut. And the nurse immediately took control. "Keep holding that," she said, pointing to the tubes in his hand. "I will be right back. Heather, hang in there." She raced out the door and in an instant her voice came over the hospital's PA system, calling for help in Heather's room. It finally sank in for Jeremy that this was the woman he'd come to see—the survivor of the helicopter crash who had, it seemed, been attacked near fatally again. *What have you gotten yourself mixed up in, Heather Sloan?*

In a flash the blonde nurse was back, followed by two other nurses in pale green scrubs. One of the new nurses glared at Jeremy for a moment, before taking the IV tubing out of his hands and holding it in place. The other nurse poked buttons on the machine on the other side of Heather's bed.

He opened his mouth to ask what he could do before realizing he was useless in a hospital. But he did know what needed to be done. With the victim secured, it was time to go after the attacker. Sprinting for the door, the voice of the other nurse stopped him. "Where do you think you're going? You can't just leave. The police will have questions for you."

"I'll have questions for them, too. As soon as I get back."

Spinning out the door, he raced toward the stairs. Someone like the man who had been in Heather's room would be noticed riding in a crowded elevator or strolling through the crowded halls of the hospital. He'd look for a deserted escape route.

Following the path Jeremy assumed the other man had taken and trying to keep his shoes from sliding on the freshly buffed floors, he skidded into the stairwell. As he raced down the steps, he tried to remember any distinguishing factors about the other man. He had been on the floor when the attacker passed, so his observations were limited, but based on the condition of the black boots he'd worn and the terrible stench that followed him around, Jeremy's best guess was that he was homeless. And his hair was silver and matted. That was a pretty slim description.

Now he could kick himself in the pants for not getting a better look at the would-be...killer? But was he really trying to kill Heather? Why else would he have put something into her IV line?

But what could their connection possibly be?

Could it be related to a case she had been working?

Four flights later he ended up in a storage room piled with stacks of clean laundry. Metal shelves lined the walls, and additional rows filled most of the floor-space, so he dropped to the ground, peering through the six-inch gap below the bottom of each shelf. Palms flat on the cold floor, he craned his neck in search of those black boots.

Satisfied that he was alone, Jeremy jumped back up and hurried to the door, which led him into a hallway next to the E.R. Straight ahead was the ambulance entrance. Stopping quickly at the nurses' station, he flashed his badge and asked, "Did you see a homeless man go past here a couple minutes ago?"

The young man behind the desk nodded. "Sure. White hair and gray jacket?" He pointed toward the glass doors. "He looked like he was in a hurry."

"Thanks." Jeremy followed the old man's path, hoping he wasn't too late.

The sun hid behind a cloud as he stepped into the fresh air, looking around the parking lot. A woman with a broken leg rolled her wheelchair past him, and a flashy black Mercedes peeled out of the visitor's parking lot. No sign of the old man.

Jeremy's shoulders sagged as he headed back into the hospital, opting this time to take the elevator instead of the stairs. Glancing at his watch, he wondered how long his useless chase had lasted. Had he missed out on clues in the hospital room that could have helped him?

As he approached Heather's room, the frantic sounds of saving a life continued. A deep voice had been added to the mix, but its tone was just as concerning as the others.

Turning away, he walked toward a small, deserted waiting room on the floor, images of Heather writhing in pain still flashing behind his closed eyelids. It was too familiar, knowing a woman was in pain and being completely helpless.

Pushing memories of the other woman out of his mind and focusing on the one he could still help, he slumped into a seat and pulled out his cell phone. Dialing an old friend, who he'd worked with on two unrelated drug cases when he started with the sheriff's department years before, he said, "Hey, Tony."

"Latham. How's everything in the sheriff's office?"

He shrugged out of habit. "Good. We're keeping busy."

"Yeah, I heard about that chopper crash. You working it?"

"Always." His experience as an FAA agent supposedly made him an asset in situations like this, but the end of his time there had made it clear that he didn't bring nearly as much to the table as the sheriff thought.

"So what can I do for you?" The tone of Tony's voice relayed that he remembered that he and the PD owed Jeremy a favor for a tip on a case two months before.

"There was a situation at Immanuel Lutheran Hospital today."

"You mean the one about five minutes ago?"

"Yes."

"How do you know about it? I'm not even sure that our guys have made it down there yet."

Jeremy ran his free hand through his wavy brown hair in desperate need of a trim. "I know. I'm here now. I was coming to talk to the crash survivor. An old guy—I think maybe homeless from the smell of him—was in her room and put something into her IV. The doctor is still working with her. I'm not sure what he dosed her with or what's really going on, but the guy got away." He couldn't keep the frustration out of his voice.

"Whoa."

"I know. So listen, I need you to do me a favor and keep your eye out at the jail just in case someone brings in a homeless guy with white hair, a gray jacket and black boots."

"But that could be anybody. How would I even know if it's your guy?" Tony sounded stumped.

"Just call me. I'll come down and check it out."

"Okay. You got it, man."

Jeremy hung up his phone and walked back toward Heather's room. The voices inside continued at a slightly less rattled pace, but Heather clearly wasn't out of danger yet.

Back pressed against the wall, Jeremy slid to the floor, adrenaline leaving his system like a flood. Resting his forearms against bent knees and his chin against his chest, he sighed. *God, please save Heather*. He barely knew the girl—hadn't even had a real conversation with her, but something was going on. And she needed all the help she could get.

* * *

Heather's eyes refused to open yet again, but for the first time in forever she felt human. The fog had lifted in her brain, and she was able to quickly take account of the situation.

The beeping monitor to her left and firm pillow beneath her head told her she was still in the hospital. Her leg still ached from the surgery.

Her shoulder felt significantly more normal than it had the last time she was awake, and a quick rotation provided only a minor twinge.

And the burning in her arm was gone. It tingled a little bit, but she couldn't be sure that wasn't just a memory of the pain of whatever had been injected into her arm.

All seemed normal. Now. But it hadn't been that way.

Before.

How long had she been asleep? When had that home-less man been in her room? What had he done to her? And why had she been his target?

Why hadn't she responded better? Years of training had gone down the tubes with a little bit of pain medication that made her feel blurry. She'd been useless. Like she had been during the crash.

A phone rang, and a hand pulled out of hers. Had someone been holding her hand? She turned her hand over, squeezing it into a loose fist, trying to recall the shape and size of the absent hand.

From the far corner of the room, came a deep voice. She recognized it, but couldn't place it.

"Nate?" she called, while trying to pry her heavy lids apart.

The voice ended suddenly before resuming by her side. "No. It's not Nate. It's Jeremy."

Finally her eyes opened, and she looked into a handsome, if only moderately familiar, face. She'd definitely seen him before, but where? Suddenly a wheezing cough racked her body. He reached for a glass and held the straw to her lips, so she could greedily sip at it. When she finally leaned back, he put the cup back on the table and scooted a chair closer to the bed.

"Jeremy Latham," he said, reading the confusion in her eyes. "I'm a deputy with the Multnomah County Sheriff's Office."

"Have we met before? You look so familiar."

He shook his head. "I've been here a couple times, but you've always been out. Except last time."

"When the homeless man was here." It was a statement, not a question, as the veil covering that memory finally lifted. She nodded slowly, but it was like trying to put a puzzle together with missing pieces. She'd lost hours…maybe even days. "When was that?"

He bit the corner of his mouth and leaned forward over his knees. "Two days ago."

"And I haven't been awake since then?"

"No." His dark curls bounced as his head moved, but his eyes remained steeled against whatever he had to say next. And she was certain there was more to come. As silence reigned, she waited. He didn't move, only stared at her with that unwavering gaze.

"So why have you been coming to see me?" A swift glance at the window proved the sun had set long before. "And after visiting hours, I'd guess." A longer look at the window, and she realized that her neck was free of the annoying brace she'd been wearing since the crash.

She tested her strength and mobility with a couple of gentle stretches.

"Are you stiff?" he asked.

"Not too bad, actually." She glared at him, then looked away, still testing the strength of her neck. "But you didn't answer my question."

He followed her gaze toward the opposite wall, as a frown punctuated his mouth. "I guess it is getting late."

"You obviously know who I am, so you must know what I do. What do you want with me?"

He tugged on the hair at his temples, his forehead wrinkling. His eyes moved back and forth, looking for anything else to focus on. "Well, as I said, I'm with the sheriff's department." He pulled out the badge attached to his belt. Probably a force of habit for him like it was for her. "I'm investigating the PNW Tourism helicopter crash."

Now it was her turn to avoid the topic at hand. "What did that man put in my IV? It burned."

"I know."

"How do you know?"

His dark brown eyes softened. "I heard you screaming."

Heat rose up her neck, and she brought her hand up to her cheek to cover the embarrassing blush. How could she have been so weak? Trying desperately to change the subject, she asked again, "So what was it?"

"That, I don't know. The doctors wouldn't tell me much. As best I can figure, it was a lethal combination of street drugs. The guys in the police lab have already started analyzing the sample, but they don't have a final report yet. You did good pulling that tube out." His admiration was genuine, and she felt the redness returning to her cheeks. When had she become such a ninny?

A yawn cracked her jaw, but for the first time since the crash, she was able to fight off the tiredness. Pressing a button on her bed elevated her head until she felt less likely to doze off in the middle of their conversation. It also added an extra measure of pressure on her leg, and she groaned.

"Is something wrong?" Jeremy's eyes filled with concern, and he reached out to touch her arm. The familiar weight of his hand gave her small start.

"Were you holding my hand?"

Now it was his turn to look embarrassed. His deep tan kept his cheeks from turning pink, but his gaze bounced around the room. "The nurse said that it's good to let someone know you're there, even if they're asleep. I was just…letting you know I was here."

"How long have you been here?"

Jeremy glanced at his watch. "Not long. A couple of hours."

She couldn't contain the snicker that came out of her mouth. "What have you been doing for a couple of hours?"

"Thinking mostly."

"About what?"

His lips pursed to the side, his eyes narrowing. "Just wondering what brought that helicopter down."

She stared directly into his eyes, wondering if they were thinking the same things about the crash. He hadn't been there, hadn't heard Kit's last words, so how could they be? But what if he had other information? He'd probably seen the helicopter after the crash. He was looking into the reasons behind it. Maybe he could be useful.

The leg in the brace spasmed violently beneath her blanket, reminding her of her own weakness. But it didn't matter. She was going to find out what happened, what caused her sister's death. After all, Heather had done nothing during the crash to save her sister. She'd been useless. And Kit deserved more than that. Solving this case was Heather's only way to begin making up for that failure.

What if she stayed away from the investigation like Nate had ordered and they never found out why Kit had lost her life? What if they lost crucial time thinking it was nothing more than an accident? What if they never named a true culprit?

Heather couldn't live with herself if she let that happen. And the only way to make sure it didn't was to do her own investigating. Kit was too important to leave it up to someone Heather didn't know.

"How much do you know about the crash?" He looked around the room, trying to keep from meeting her gaze, so she pushed again. "I'm a big girl. I deserve to know the truth, don't you think?"

A little wobble of his head followed his shrug. Still not looking into her eyes, he said, "My contact at the FAA says it looks like the wires to the cyclic were disengaged."

"The cyclic?"

"The joystick-type thing that controls the helicopter. It's called a cyclic, and the wires to it appeared to be partially severed."

The pilot had said something about the cyclic losing power, hadn't he? Apparently Jeremy knew about helicopters, and he had a contact with the FAA. Two things she didn't have. Yes, he could definitely be useful.

But how to get him to share his information? The

sheriff's office probably wouldn't like an FBI agent poking around in the case…especially since she didn't actually have authorization from the FBI to investigate.

She choked on an unexpected breath, at the memory of Nate's last words to her. She was supposed to let Deputy Latham and the FAA do the investigating on this case.

Not likely.

That was her sister who had been buried. And she wasn't going to back away quietly. No matter what Nate said.

He just didn't need to know. Which meant he didn't need to know about the attack by the homeless man either. He'd go into overprotective mode and insist on having her guarded around the clock. She'd never get any investigating done that way.

"What are you thinking about the crash? Do you think those wires were cut on purpose? Was the chopper sabotaged?" she finally asked.

As though she hadn't asked the last questions, he said, "I'm wondering why that homeless man was in here. Targeting you."

"I've been wondering the same thing."

"Did he say anything?"

Heather dove into the foggy recesses of her mind until she could see and almost smell the man next to her bed. His lips moved, but what had he said? "Put the tube in the line. Get the fix."

"Put the tube in the line? Get the fix? As in put the tube of drugs in your IV line and he'd get a fix?"

"His hands were shaking really badly. He had to have been in withdrawal. Someone must have told him that if he gave me the overdose, they would get him more drugs."

Jeremy nodded in agreement. "That sounds about right."

A coughing fit caught her off guard, and she wrapped her arms around her middle. The searing pain in her shoulder as she tried to reach for the water cup on her bedside table made her groan, and Jeremy jumped to help her.

"Here. Drink this." He pressed the straw to her lips, and she gulped greedily. His hands belonged to someone who worked hard, and she studied his knuckles, worn and weathered. "Better?" he asked, pulling the straw away, but keeping it at the ready in case she needed another swallow.

"I think so." She only managed a mumble, angry with her inability to care for herself. Her knee throbbed, and suddenly she ached all over. Bruises that she'd successfully ignored until now screamed at her. And her brain nearly mutinied under the pressure that was growing beneath her temples.

What if she couldn't do it? What if she couldn't figure out what had happened? What if she physically could not bring the person responsible for Kit's death to justice?

If she couldn't solve the case, she didn't deserve to be an FBI agent. And she certainly didn't deserve to be part of her family. A family still in mourning.

Until she brought justice to Kit's killer, she didn't deserve to grieve. And if she never grieved, her heart might never heal.

Latham had leaned back in his chair, his gaze thoughtful, arms folded across his chest. His eyes seemed to look right through her, focused on an unseen target. Heather recognized the look on his face. She'd seen it from Nate and Myles, another FBI coworker. She'd probably even made it herself a few times. He was solving a case deep in his mind.

And if she didn't join him, she'd fall too far behind to ever take the lead.

With a bum leg and strict orders to steer clear of the investigation, cutting herself off from most of her resources, she'd never crack the case on her own. At least with him, she'd have access to all of his connections, research and mobility.

And he needed her. Needed her insight into Kit, and what she said after the helicopter went down. They could help each other.

Suddenly she wanted to tell Latham everything she knew. Tell him about the crash and Kit's worries. Tell him that she knew the helicopter going down wasn't an accident. But what if he wasn't willing to help her? What if he didn't want an injured agent trailing after him for weeks or maybe months? She had to get his word, had to get him to agree.

Swallowing thickly, she closed her eyes for a moment. "There's more," she said.

"What is it?" He leaned forward, his elbows resting on his knees, an eager light filling his eyes.

"First I have to get your word that you'll help me."

His eyebrows clenched together, and he sat back into his chair. "Are you in trouble?"

"Not the way that you mean. My sister died in that crash."

"I know, and I'm sorry."

Heather swallowed again, the sound seeming to fill the whole room. "I owe it to her to see this investigation through. I need to know what happened, I need to know who's responsible."

His face relaxed. "Sure. I'll keep you in the loop every step."

"That's not enough. I want to be at the front of the investigation."

He glanced at the enormous brace covering her leg, and when his gaze lifted, his eyes filled with bewilderment as he let out a disbelieving laugh. "You're kidding, right? How could you possibly be on the ground investigating? You're not exactly mobile."

"I know," she conceded. "That's why I'll need your help. You could help me get around, take me whenever you're going to be looking into anything related to the crash. In exchange, I'll give you all the details from the crash, and tell you anything you want to know about my sister."

"So you think the crash had something to do with your sister?"

"I'm sure of it." She reached out to touch him, ignoring the sting in her shoulder. His forearm jumped when her fingers brushed the dark hairs growing there. "I can help you. I *need* to help you."

He scrubbed open palms over his face, eyes still squinting. "No. You need to be at home recovering. You've been through a traumatic experience. I get that."

"No, you don't! What would you do if it was your sister?" Desperation made her voice jump half an octave, and she took a calming breath.

His nose wrinkled as he took a deep breath as well. Something like regret flickered across his face and disappeared in an instant. "I understand. Please trust me. I do. But this isn't healthy for you, physically or emotionally. You need to recuperate. Do something to keep your mind off your sister."

"Like helping you with the investigation."

His shoulders rose and fell, but the sigh was silent. "Like reading a book."

"Please. I can help you. I have information that might be helpful."

Frown lines crinkled around his eyes. "You know I could arrest you for hindering an ongoing investigation if you don't tell me what you know, if you don't share with me whatever it is that makes you so sure this crash was about your sister."

"I know. But I also know that you need me. And I need you."

He stood, pacing the small room with purposeful strides. "I just don't know." He sighed, running long fingers through his hair. Head bowed, he turned slightly to look at her.

"I know what I'm asking. I know it won't be easy. For either of us. But I have to do this for my sister. And you need the information that I have. Besides, when I tell you what I know, I think you're going to have a bigger case than you realize."

"But you've just been through major surgery."

"I'm also a special agent with the FBI. I can handle this. I won't slow you down. Much."

"Why don't you just ask your friends in the Bureau to get involved?" he asked. "I bet they'd work with you. Give you the information you want. Help you launch your own investigation."

"I can't." She couldn't hold his gaze when she continued. "My Special Agent in Charge told me to rest. He ordered me to stay out of it."

Latham's face turned smug. "Smart guy. Listen to him."

She squinted at him, praying that he would understand

her heart in just that moment. She'd been broken. This was her only hope at healing. "You know I can't. Let me help you. We'll solve this case together."

He remained silent for several moments, running his palms over his cheeks and stretching his facial skin. Finally he nodded. "All right. Tell me what you know."

Swallowing the lump in her throat and pushing the pain in her heart to the side, Heather said, "Kit was a Deputy D.A. here in Portland. She handled some pretty major cases."

"I know."

"After the chopper crashed, Kit was still conscious." Jeremy suddenly looked very interested. Sliding back into the plastic chair, he leaned closer. "She told me—" Heather swallowed thickly again, blinking away the moisture threatening to pool in the corners of her eyes. "Just before she died, she told me…to follow the drugs."

"What drugs?"

"I'm not sure. Maybe she was getting ready to prosecute a case involving drugs. But whatever drugs she was talking about, she believed they had something to do with the crash. She was convinced of it or she wouldn't have said anything. I'm sure of it."

"So you think the chopper was tampered with to cause a crash to kill your sister so she couldn't prosecute this case?"

"Yes."

He nodded, but his face remained unreadable. "What about you? Do you think that poisoning attack with the IV was connected to Kit's case?"

"Well, it could be a coincidence that a guy stumbled into my hospital room and tried to kill me with a mess of street drugs while talking about getting his own fix just five days after I almost died in a crash—a crash that killed my sister, who believed the reason behind the crash was illegal drugs."

"But…"

"But I don't believe in coincidences."

"Me, neither." His eyes turned a softer shade of brown, and he squeezed her hand. "You're in some serious trouble."

THREE

"Mom, I'm fine. Really. You can take off. Nora is going to come by and check on me every day after work."

"But what about during the day? What if you need something? Shouldn't I stay a little longer?"

Heather looked into green eyes so much like Kit's, and a pang of sadness shot through her stomach. She almost dropped the half smile she'd pasted on her face. Reaching for her mom's hand, she squeezed it gently. "I'm okay. I have crutches to get around the apartment. A couple kids from the church youth group are going to pick up food and groceries for me. There's really nothing else I need. I'm really glad that you came, but you have a life back in Sacramento."

And I have a case to solve.

Her mom's gray hair bobbed around her ears, as she gave her oldest daughter a solid once-over. "I wish your dad didn't have to get back to the base to get his unit ready to deploy. He'd talk you into letting us stay."

The corner of Heather's mouth lifted slowly. "No he wouldn't. He'd tell you that you raised a tough girl and that I'll never get better if you coddle me."

Her mom nodded and chuckled. "You're probably right."

Heather's eyes locked with her mom's, and she squeezed the older woman's hand. "I love you. Both of you."

"We love you, too, sweetie." Her mom leaned down to kiss the top of Heather's head, softly patting her hair. "If you need me, just call. I don't mind coming back. Whatever you need."

"Have a safe flight. Thanks!" Heather called from her seat on the couch, just before her mom disappeared behind the closed door. Her leg propped on the cushions beside her and head resting on the back of the sofa, she stared at the ceiling. She'd been home from the hospital just two days, but already the walls were beginning to close in.

She had to get out of the condo and start working on the case. Thinking about Kit's killer walking around free was driving her crazy. The trouble was she hadn't heard from Jeremy since he'd agreed to help her.

Apparently she was going to have to make the first move. Reaching for her phone, she nearly rolled off the couch when it rang at ear-piercing volume before she touched it. Apparently her mom thought her injury also made her deaf.

"Sloan."

"Well, that's some greeting," said the voice on the other end of the line.

"Nate? What's going on?"

Her supervisor's tone was a little too light when he said, "Just calling to check on you. Nora said I have to make sure that you're doing okay, especially since your mom left today."

"She's been gone literally five minutes. I'm fine."

She sounded grumpier than she meant to, but something told her he wasn't just calling to check in. "Now spill it. Why'd you really call?"

In typical Nate fashion, he switched topics the moment the questions were directed at him. "I talked with personnel today. You're going to have to be inactive with the Bureau for anywhere from six weeks to three months."

"Three months! You're kidding, right?" He was teasing. He had to be. There was no way she could spend three months on the couch. At least she'd have time to wrap up Kit's case.

"Sorry, kid. It might only be a few weeks, but you'll have to do a lot of physical therapy and then be cleared by the doctor to be reinstated."

But what if the case wrapped up in just a few weeks? How would she fill her three months then? "Can't I at least get behind a desk? I can still do paperwork. I have two fully—well, mostly—functioning arms. I can write reports. Do research. Man the phones. Whatever you need. I just can't sit on a couch for that long."

"I know this isn't any fun. It's not fun for me either. I'm going to have to put up with the coffee that Myles or James makes for who knows how long. That's just rotten. I may even have to go out looking for a new barista agent for the office just to get some good joe."

Heather knew her laugh was exactly what he wanted, but she couldn't hold it back. "Or you could make your own coffee."

"What's the point of being the SAC if I have to make it myself?"

Just in case they were on the edge of getting too familiar, every so often, Nate would throw out a reminder that he was the Special Agent in Charge of the Portland office. "As always, excellent point, sir."

"Nice try. No amount of brownnosing is going to get you behind a desk any sooner." He paused, and she could almost see his face turning serious. "Just take care of yourself, okay? Lay low. Get some rest, and get healed. We need you back in the office. Functioning at a hundred percent."

"Sure. Okay." *Or not so much.*

"I'm serious, Sloan." His tone took on a quality not unlike her mom's angry voice.

"Yes, sir. I'll keep my head down and I won't take any unnecessary chances with my health." *And that's the truth. Any risks I take to find Kit's killer are entirely necessary.*

"Good. Nora will be by tonight. She broke our date to make sure you're okay. I hope you appreciate the pain that I'm going through so my fiancée can check up on you."

She chuckled again before hanging up. She could feel the weight of exhaustion pulling at her. The drugs made her so groggy, but she couldn't seem to sleep soundly. Maybe a nap would help.

Immediately her phone rang again, and she nearly chucked it across the room, which would have been torture to retrieve. Fumbling it between stiff fingers, she managed to flip it back open. "Yes?" she said, nearly out of breath.

"Heather?"

"Yes."

"It's Latham—sorry—Jeremy."

"Do you have any news?"

He paused for a moment, and she thought she could hear a voice coming through the radio in his car. "I just got a call from my friend Tony with the Portland P.D. He thinks there may be a body in the morgue that's of interest to us."

"Really? How so?"

"I'm not sure. He just said there's a guy there I should see. The last time I talked to Tony was right after you were poisoned in the hospital."

"You think it's connected?"

"It's worth checking out. Where do you live? I'm coming to get you."

"But I was just—" She stopped herself. She was the one who had asked him for help. Just because her eyelids drooped and her brain called for a rest, didn't mean she had to give in to them. "I live off of Fifth." She quickly gave him directions to her town house.

"I'm not far. I'll be there in about five minutes."

She looked down at her jeans, one leg split to the top of the gray brace, and faded blue T-shirt. She wasn't sure she could muster the energy required to change clothes, so she looked around for a sweater or something to pull over the old shirt. Finally she grabbed her crutches from where they rested against the head of the couch. Pulling herself carefully to one foot, she moved slowly across the room to her bedroom. A black pullover sweater lay on the foot of the bed, and she leaned against the mattress to pull it on.

Just as she finished adjusting it, loud thuds landed on her front door.

"Coming." Heather's voice sounded on the other side of the door as Jeremy tapped his foot on the cement step. There were only a handful of steps, but he wondered how she had managed to make it up them. Moreover, how was she going to make it back down?

For about the hundredth time, he questioned his decision to bring her in on the investigation. Yes, he sympathized with her loss, with her sense of helplessness—sympathized more than she knew—but was she really up for this.

"You okay in there?" he asked.

"Yes," she yelped, as she swung the door open. Her blue eyes eclipsed her pale face, and wild, yellow curls broke loose from her ponytail, framing her cheeks. Then she turned and looked at the kitchen counter on the other side of the living room. "I forgot my keys." She made a move to go for them, but he stopped her with a hand on her shoulder.

"Let me." He crossed the room, snatched the small key ring from the counter and handed them to her as he stepped back outside. "Ready?"

She followed him out the door, then turned to lock it. He watched as she took the first clattering step, analyzing her movements. Given the way her arms maneuvered the metal supports, he'd bet that normally she was pretty graceful, but the enormous brace and crutches made every motion awkward. It was entertaining to see her mulish determination to master the steps…but on the other hand, they *were* on a tight schedule.

Glancing down at his watch, he said, "The morgue closes in thirty minutes."

"I'm hurrying."

He chuckled to himself before jogging back up the steps, tucking his arm around her waist and swinging her crutches over his forearm. "Hang on," he said, as he scooped her up. Her arm immediately wrapped around his neck, like she was trying to choke him. "Maybe not quite so tight."

She blushed, moving her arm to his shoulder, as he

maneuvered them back to the street and the cruiser parked at the curb.

"Be glad all you got was an arm around the neck." Her tone was only half joking, and he took the hint. He wasn't going to be able to push her around.

Her body stayed rigid until he set her gently on one foot as he opened the back door. "I think you'll have to sit in the back. I doubt your leg will fit in the front seat."

"You're probably right." She sighed, as he helped her scoot across the seat, keeping her injured leg elevated.

As he pulled out into traffic, he glanced in his rear-view mirror. "How are you feeling today?"

"Fine, I guess." She slumped against the back of the seat with her shoulder, and her nose crinkled in distaste. "It smells bad back here."

"Sorry about that. I guess I've had some unruly guys back there lately."

"Is that what you normally do? Lock up the bad guys in the back of your car?"

He laughed loudly, resting one arm on the center console. "I am a sheriff's deputy. It pretty much comes with the job."

She seemed content to ignore his last comment and stared out the window as they moved from residential neighborhoods to a more commercial area. She crossed her arms over her chest, and he could almost see the barrier she pulled around herself. He knew that pose, that need to put up a shield so no one else could see the pain. He'd been there. Pulled his own shields so close he'd nearly cut everyone else out of his life.

He hadn't lost his sister, but he knew what it was like to lose a loved one—a fiancée. Only in his case, it had been his own fault.

As he pulled past the police station and into the parking lot reserved for cops, he shot up a quick prayer for the woman in the backseat. *Heavenly Father, would You please comfort Heather? I don't know how much help I can be, but if there's something I should say, give me the words.*

He turned off the car and jumped out from behind the wheel. When he swung the back door open, he leaned one arm on the roof and ducked his head into the car. "You ready for this?"

She wiggled along the seat, always keeping her leg carefully protected. "Of course."

She reached the edge of the seat before he remembered that he'd picked up a present for her. "I almost forgot! Sit tight." He jogged to the trunk of the car and popped it open.

"What is it?" she called.

He put the wheels on the ground, closed the trunk and ran back to stand in front of her. "Your chariot, madam." He offered an awful British accent and some silly hand flourishes to present the old wheelchair that he'd borrowed from the sheriff's office.

He wasn't sure if it was the chair or his strange behavior that made her smile, but he took an uncanny joy in watching her face change and her lips curve upward. Her eyes softened, and she held out one hand. He clasped her wrist and pulled her to her feet, helping her spin on one foot and settle into the creaking leather seat.

After propping her foot on the leg rest, he pushed her toward the small building next to the police department and held the door open for her as she rolled into the office. Flashing his badge at the man behind the front desk, he said, "Deputy Latham with the sheriff's office. The medical examiner is expecting us."

The bald man nodded toward a clipboard on the counter, waited until Jeremy signed it and turned back to his computer without a word.

Jeremy returned to Heather, pushing the wheelchair down a long hallway. They stopped at a large set of double silver doors, and Jeremy pushed one open, poking his head in.

"Rob?" He stepped farther into the bright room that broke every stereotype for a morgue. "You in here?"

"In the back. I'll be right there." The voice came from the other side of a mostly closed door, which probably led to a storage closet. Sure enough, just as he wheeled Heather through the door, Dr. Robertson walked into the room carrying several boxes. His white eyebrows rose halfway up his forehead when his eyes landed on Heather, but he didn't say anything.

Jeremy offered quick introductions. "Heather this is Dr. Robertson, M.E.—Rob, this is FBI Special Agent Heather Sloan."

Heather shot Jeremy an annoyed glance, but offered Rob a gentle smile as she held out her hand. "Rob Robertson?"

"Nope." He offered a Cheshire cat grin as he tucked his thumbs beneath his ever-present suspenders.

"No one knows his first name," Jeremy filled in at Heather's wrinkled forehead and pursed lips.

"A man of mystery. I like it." Then her smile dazzled, white teeth flashing in the bright lights. "So, Dr. Rob. Jeremy tells me that you have something that might be of interest."

"Well, Special Agent Sloan—"

"Oh, no," she cut him off. "There's no need to be so formal. Call me Heather."

Rob smiled like he'd never been in the presence of

anyone so charming before, and Jeremy had to hand it to the woman. She had brought them right where she wanted to be without having to answer any questions about her leg or why the FBI might have an interest in the man on the slab.

"All right, Heather." Rob cleared his throat and tipped his head toward a gurney behind him. "That guy was brought in four days ago. He was classified as a John Doe, and the city requires that I determine a probable cause of death for any unidentified bodies.

"I ran a tox screen and came up with a concoction of street drugs that I've never seen in almost twenty years with the city."

Reminding them that he wasn't invisible, Jeremy asked, "What made you tip us off?"

Rob did indeed look surprised when his gaze jumped back to Jeremy. "I ran the drug mix by the boys in the lab upstairs. They said your friend Tony Bianchi had dropped off an identical sample just the day before."

Jeremy glanced at Heather out of the corner of his eye, instantly catching her sideways peek. She nodded at him, and he knew they were thinking the same thing. They didn't even have to look under the sheet to identify the dead man.

"Where'd you get that sample you gave to Tony?" Rob asked.

Jeremy shrugged in response, but it was Heather who took control of the conversation again. "I think we should see if we recognize him."

Rob immediately turned his attention to Heather, apparently forgetting the question that he'd just asked. "Are you sure? He's been dead awhile, and he was on the street at least overnight."

Holding out her hand to the doctor, she said, "I'm sure. Will you help me up?"

Jeremy flipped the brake on the old chair and offered her his arm as well. She placed her left hand on his forearm and held fast. When Rob pulled the sheet back to uncover the pale face and ragged features of an old man with long, matted silver hair, Heather's grip intensified for a moment, but her face never flickered. She squeezed again, as if confirming that she knew this man.

The old man's face wasn't familiar to Jeremy, but that wasn't surprising. He'd only seen the back of the homeless man's head that day in the hospital.

"You know him?" Rob asked them both.

"I think so," Heather responded. "When did he die?"

"It's hard to pinpoint exactly, as he was in the elements for at least one night. But as close as I can tell, five days."

"And where was he found?" Jeremy offered this question, hoping Rob would answer it even if it didn't come from Heather, his new favorite person.

"About two blocks east of Immanuel Lutheran."

FOUR

"I know what you're thinking." Heather stared at Jeremy through the reflection in the rearview mirror. "Just say it." He shook his head before letting off the brake and easing through the four-way stop.

Well, if he wouldn't verbalize it, she would.

"Whoever hired that John Doe to kill me, killed him to keep him quiet."

Not meeting her eyes again, Jeremy nodded. "Why would someone be after you?"

"I don't know." She shook her head and closed her eyes. Leaning back, she tried to relieve some of the pressure in her head by rubbing slow circles in front of her ears.

"Are you sure this is all related to Kit's drug case? Were *you* working on any cases that this could be linked to?"

"No. I've been on desk duty for months. I had hip surgery, and I'd just been given the go-ahead to return to regular duty when I took a couple days off to spend some time with my si-ister."

She hated that her voice broke. Hated that tears threatened every time she even thought about Kit. The ache in her heart felt like it would never subside, never even dim.

He cleared his throat, keeping his head facing forward, as he turned on to her street. "Which hip?"

"Hmm?"

"Which hip? The same one as your knee?"

She let a soft sigh escape. "Thankfully not."

After parking the car and walking around to her door, he cocked his head to the side, as if asking permission to assist her. She lifted her hand to wave him off, but thought better of it and offered him a quick nod.

As his broad arms wrapped around her waist to help her out of the car, she braced her hands on his shoulders, admitting that once upon a time being this close to a handsome man might have sent her heart racing. But it kept a steady rhythm, just another indication of its brokenness.

He handed her the crutches and walked behind her as they made their way toward her home. She unlocked the door and shuffled through, making a beeline for the couch, immediately propping her throbbing leg on the pillow.

Jeremy followed her in, closing the door behind him and perching on the edge of the overstuffed chair near the foot of the couch.

"Listen, Heather. I'm worried about you." He rubbed his hands over his face, ruffling the short curls at his forehead.

"I can take care of myself."

He shook his head. "I know you can. I saw you in there with Dr. Rob."

"What's that supposed to mean?" She tried to keep the pleasure out of her voice. He might have meant to chide her, but she took it as a compliment to be recognized for controlling the conversation as she had.

He let out a soft laugh, meeting her eyes with humor. "Let's just say, I think I could learn a few things from you."

"Thank you."

"You're welcome. But that doesn't change the fact that someone is after you, and you're not…shall we say, moving at your normal speed?"

She crossed her arms in front of her and glared at him. "I can get around just fine."

"Is that with or without the wheelchair?"

Her lip curled, and she glared at him, wishing he would go. Wishing he were wrong. He didn't say anything, just held her gaze with a look of assurance. "Fine. All right. Maybe I'm not at normal speed. But I'm perfectly capable of taking care of myself."

"Against someone who's sending people to kill you? And then killing the would-be assassins?"

She groaned, covering her face with her hands and shaking her hair over her shoulders. "Let's just say I conceded the point. What can we do about it?"

"You need someone with you twenty-four seven."

"Like a bodyguard?" She shook her head.

His head rocked side to side, lips pursed to the left. "More like a deputy protector."

"Nope. No way." She shook her head violently, lowering her hands to look into his brown eyes. "You're out of your mind. We already agreed that you'd take me along to investigate the crash, so I'll already be with you most of the time."

"Yes. But this way, I'll tag along wherever you're going outside of the investigation, too."

Was he serious? "What on earth do you think you can do that I can't?"

"This very moment? Run. Walk normally. Drive a car."

She harrumphed and tried to seriously injure him with her eyes, but his annoying smirk stayed in place. Why did he have to make so much sense? She wanted to do this on her own. As much as she could while recovering from major surgery and without the aide of her Bureau connections. Having to count on him to help figure out why the chopper went down was bad enough. Letting him tag along on every errand? Unacceptable.

"If I say no?"

"I'll take care of the investigation on my own."

"But we had a deal."

"The rules changed." He rubbed his palms over his knees. "I'm not saying that watching you try to maneuver those crutches isn't painful even for me, but I don't want to see you killed, either. What if your sister had more info than we know now? I might need some help getting ahold of that. I need you around." His mouth quirked into half a smile, and she knew he was teasing her.

She punched the pillow supporting her back. "Can't we just agree that I won't leave my home without telling you?"

Jeremy lifted his hands in what she quickly realized was a faux surrender. "Sure. We'll just leave a note for the perp that you'll be home alone from eleven to eight every night." He rested his hands on his knees and leaned toward her. "He knew where to find you at the hospital. I'm not willing to bet that he doesn't know where you live."

A chill ran across her shoulders, and despite the scowl

she gave Jeremy, she knew he was right. She might need more protection than she could give herself at the moment. And no matter what, she couldn't risk Jeremy backing out of their agreement to let her help with the investigation.

Resigning herself to the inevitable, she grumbled, "All right."

He smiled. "Great. When should I move my stuff in?"

She nearly choked on a simple inhaled breath, coughing making her double over in pain. Jeremy leaned in and patted her back. She sucked air into her lungs between gasps, never taking her eyes off his impish grin.

When she could finally speak, she muttered, "What do you mean move your stuff in? You can't stay here."

"Of course I can." His tone turned firm, less jovial. "You need someone with you all day every day. I happen to be available."

"Don't you have anything better to do with your evenings other than babysitting me? Friends you want to spend time with? Family? Girlfriend?"

Pain flashed across his expression for a moment, instantly making her feel guilty. Clearly she'd hit a raw nerve. "I…I didn't mean to…" Her voice trailed off. He was kind enough to ignore the half-hearted apology.

"Listen, Heather," he said, all humor gone from his face. "I know this is tough for you, but I'm not going to let you stay alone."

"But I barely know you!"

"Ask me anything you want. I'll tell you whatever you need to know. So you pretty much have two options. Me…" He pointed his thumb at his chest and quirked one eyebrow. "Or someone from the Bureau. Your call.

But I'm not about to leave you on your own to face who knows what's out there."

"Ugh." She turned, crossed her arms and looked away from Jeremy as he leaned back into the chair, already too much at home. He knew she couldn't go to her office for help without revealing what she was up to.

His grin returned full-force. "Good. I'll pick up my stuff tonight." Pulling out a little notebook from his pocket, he asked, "So where do you think we should start?"

Without even a thought about what he was asking, she said, "Kit's office."

His forehead wrinkled, and his dark eyebrows pulled together. "What about the wreckage from the crash? There isn't someone responsible if it was an accident. Shouldn't we start there, to confirm that the cyclic controls were actually tampered with?"

"If it was an accident, then why is someone trying to take me out of the picture?"

He pursed his lips. "Valid point. But are we certain that it's not related to a past case of yours?"

"It's not. I just know it. Kit said to follow the drugs." Heather swallowed loudly.

"But if we wait to investigate the wreckage, evidence may disappear."

She hated that he made sense. Why did he have to be good at his job and so frustrating at the same time?

"What if we have to know what Kit knew to make any sense of the crash or the rest of the investigation? Shouldn't we start there?"

He stared straight at her injured leg for several long seconds, pressing his fingers together, making a triangle with his thumbs. "Fine. We'll start with Kit's office in the morning. But then we're immediately going to check out the chopper."

She nodded. "Good."

Suddenly her front door vibrated under the force of three solid thumps.

"Are you expecting anyone?"

She shook her head, her heart already in her throat.

Jeremy jumped, reaching under his jacket and adjusting his shoulder holster. Just as he reached the door, Heather chuckled.

"I just realized that assassins don't usually knock."

He laughed, too, as he peered through the peephole. She had a good point. Still, it wouldn't hurt to be cautious. A man with dark hair stood with his hands shoved into the pockets of black slacks. "Can I help you?" Jeremy asked after cracking the door open.

"Who are you?" the other man demanded, leaning in toward the door and trying to push past Jeremy's firm stance.

He couldn't help the scowl that followed the man's rudeness. "I could ask you the same question."

"I'm Clay Kramer." The man's eyes turned to slits, his gaze never wavering. "Where is Heather? If you've hurt her, I'll—"

"Clay, it's okay!" Heather yelled from the couch. "Jeremy, let him in."

A quick glance over his shoulder proved that Heather was indeed as exasperated as her voice sounded. Reluctantly Jeremy stepped back; Kramer just a blur as he ran into the room and straight for Heather. Kramer's suit wrinkled as he knelt before the suddenly teary-eyed Heather, who wrapped her arms around the intruder and tucked her face into his neck.

Why hadn't she told Jeremy that she had a boyfriend? It seemed like it should have come up in their discussion about his staying on her couch.

A jealous boyfriend was exactly what he didn't need to get this case solved. He'd be slowed down, and Heather would inevitably be distracted. And those were absolutely the only reasons why he felt something drop in the pit of his stomach at the sight of Heather nestling so naturally in another man's arms.

He shook his head and swallowed the growl that threatened low in his throat. Shoving his hands deep into his pockets, he strolled back to the chair he'd just vacated as the reunion embrace finally ended.

Kramer pulled back, Heather's hands cupping his cheeks, holding him close. "I am so sorry. I tried to save her."

"I know you did, sweetie." His hand ran over the top of her blond waves.

Please don't let them kiss.

Jeremy wasn't sure he could handle it just then.

Seeing couples in love always reminded him of the woman he'd planned to share his life with. Of course, it had been awhile since he'd shared a kiss with her, but the memory of Reena's touch was like a punch to the gut. Fighting the urge to wallow in the misery of her memory, he turned his attention back to the lovebirds.

Except…they weren't kissing. They weren't even touching anymore. And instead of happiness on her face, Heather just looked sad. Sadder than before Kramer's arrival.

As Jeremy studied the planes of her face, she glanced up, surprise lighting her eyes. Had she forgotten he was even there?

"Oh! Jeremy." Kramer turned toward him at her outburst. "I'm sorry. This is Clay."

"We've met."

A half smile danced across her face. "Of course. Clay is… I mean, he was…"

Clay offered Heather a pat on her shoulder before finishing her sentence. "Heather's sister and I were engaged. The wedding was set for next month."

Too many times to remember Jeremy had been on the giving end of bad news because of his job. He'd received his fair share of it, too. But he still never knew how to respond. *I'm sorry* seemed trite. *I'm sure it will get easier* diminished the family's pain. Not saying anything at all was cold.

And he wanted to be anything but cold toward Heather, as pain filled every feature of her face. Tiny wrinkles at the corner of her mouth appeared as she swallowed quickly. Young eyes suddenly looked far too old, and as her fingers moved to brush at her eyelashes, they shook.

Had he been wrong to agree to let her work the case with him? Could she handle the day-to-day strain of the investigation?

Still unsure what to say, he remained mute.

In the end Heather saved him from having to say anything at all, clearing her throat to fill the silence. With a quick blink and audible swallow, she composed herself. "Clay, I'm sorry I wasn't at the funeral."

He nodded. "I understand."

"It's just that the doctors didn't know when I would be out of the hospital. And my dad had to leave. And they didn't even tell me about it until afterward. And…"

Kramer put his hand on her shoulder, squeezing his

thumb into the soft fabric of her sweater. "I get it. Kit would have, too."

Heather opened her mouth to say something, but a light knock on the door interrupted whatever was on her mind.

Jeremy strode to the door, peering again through the hole. This time a pretty blonde woman stood on the other side. He opened it wider than he had for Kramer and smiled at her obvious surprise.

"Oh! I'm Nora. I'm looking for Heather." Her gaze flitted around the door frame as though trying to confirm that she was indeed at the right house.

"She's right inside." He nodded over his shoulder and stepped back to let her enter.

"I guess you already have a full house," Nora chirped, as she strolled across the room. Lifting the casserole dish in her hands, she smiled. "I just thought I'd bring you a lasagna. It's all ready to go. Just bake it."

Heather managed a pained grimace toward her friend, who returned from putting the meal in the refrigerator, clearly curious about the two men as she looked back and forth between them.

Heather made quick introductions, her voice wavering only slightly when she introduced Clay. Nora's face lost all color, then red spots appeared on the apples of her cheeks as she shook Clay's hand in both of hers. "Yes, of course. We didn't have a chance to meet at the funeral. I'm so sorry for your loss," she said.

Jeremy stayed near the door, unsure how he fit into the little group at the couch. At once fiercely protective of his new partner, and also just an outsider with no attachment to Kit. His interest was purely in terms of solving the case.

After a few minutes of quiet conversation, Nora

took her leave. She squeezed Heather in a tight hug, and stepped toward the door. "I'll see you tomorrow."

Heather shook her head quickly. "There's no need for you stop by every day. I'm doing fine."

"But I don't mind, really. I want to help out."

Clay rested his hand on Heather's shoulder. "She won't be alone. I'll be here as much as she needs me."

Jeremy stepped forward to stake his own claim to her time, but paused at the nearly imperceptible raise of Heather's eyebrows. He stopped and shrugged to let her know he understood. But he wasn't quite sure he did.

"Are you sure you don't need me tomorrow? I can bring over dinner again."

Heather smiled. "I can't possibly finish that lasagna in one day. I'll be fine. I promise." Holding up three fingers, she gave a mock scout salute. "I'll call if I need anything."

Nora tilted her head, as if trying to tell if Heather was really speaking the truth. "All right. But call me if you change your mind. It's no problem for me to swing by on my way home from work."

"Thank you," Heather said, as the petite woman strode to the door. Jeremy held it open for her and received a smile as she stepped outside.

When he turned back to the scene in the center of the room, Clay was kneeling next to Heather, holding both of her hands in his.

"Did Kit say anything before she died?" Clay asked softly.

Heather's lips trembled, and she finally bit on the lower one. "I'm sorry. She didn't." She looked away, then back at the other man. "It all happened so fast. She was gone so fast."

Clay cleared his throat and ran one of his hands

through his overly styled hair. "I'm sorry to ask you to relive it."

Heather managed another wobbly smile, and Jeremy took that as his cue to give them some privacy. He cleared his throat as he opened the door, and two sets of eyes focused on him. "I'm just going to run over to my place and pick up a few things. I'll be back in about half an hour." Then just for Heather, "You'll be okay until then?"

She nodded. "I'm good."

Clay, on the other hand, looked like he'd swallowed a bug. His pale blue gaze jumping back and forth between them, he asked, "What's going on?" His shoulders squared into a definitively older brother posture. Jabbing his thumb in Jeremy's direction, he spoke directly to Heather. "Is this guy staying here with you?"

Jeremy shrugged as he slipped out the door. Heather could deal with Clay like she'd dealt with Dr. Rob.

At least as long as Clay was there, Heather wasn't alone if someone made another attempt on her life.

FIVE

Heather stumbled into the kitchen in search of the pot to start some coffee, only to find the pot brewed and already half-empty. Flinging open the cupboard door on the hunt for her favorite mug and finding it missing made her grumble.

"Morning, sunshine."

Brushing a wayward lock of hair out of her face with her forearm and balancing on one crutch, she glared at Latham. Relaxed at the kitchen table and drinking out of *her* blue-and-white-polka-dot cup, he peered over the top of the newspaper.

"You're drinking out of my mug."

His chocolate eyes flicked toward the cup in his right hand. "Sorry. I didn't know they were assigned."

"Well, they are." He laughed, and she steamed.

Holding it out at arm's length, he asked, "Do you want it back?"

"No. Just make sure it's clean tomorrow morning."

He chuckled again before diving behind his paper, a damp curl falling across his forehead. He had already cleaned up and was wearing a wrinkle-free, blue button-down. "What time did you get up?" she asked, resuming her hunt in the cupboard.

"A while ago. I'm a morning person."

"Of course you're a morning person," she grumbled, filling her mug to the brim. Taking a sip, she nearly spit it right back out. "What is this?"

Setting his paper down and taking a gulp of coffee, he shrugged. "It's a dark roast. Why?" Then as understanding crossed his face, "I like it a little strong."

Her face contorted in pain. "That's nearly a solid!"

This made him chuckle again. "It helps wake me up a little faster." As she poured out about a third of the coffee in the cup into the sink and filled it back up with hot water, he mumbled something she couldn't quite make out that sounded an awful lot like, "Apparently I'm the only morning person here."

"Well, maybe I'd be more of a morning person, if I'd been able to get more than thirty minutes of sleep last night. As it was, even through the closed door, your snoring kept me up to all hours."

He looked genuinely affronted. "I don't snore. I don't think." Looking toward the ceiling as though thinking it through, he continued. "My college roommates never complained. Course they snored, too."

Heather shook her head and took another drink of the now palatable java. "I'm going to go get ready, and do my physical therapy." Her crutches clicked on the tile floor with every step. "I'll be ready to go to Kit's office in about forty-five minutes."

His drying curls danced as he nodded. "Sure thing. Do you need any help with your therapy?"

She shot him a withering glare.

"All right. That's a no." He fought to keep the crooked grin from reappearing. "Can I make you something for breakfast?"

"I'll grab a doughnut before we leave," she said before closing her bedroom door on him.

True to her word, she emerged dressed and ready to head out the door—albeit with a tender knee—less than an hour later. Latham perched on the edge of the couch next to a pile of neatly folded blankets and pillows, his black cell phone tucked between his ear and his shoulder as he scribbled onto a hand-size notepad.

"Got it. Thanks, Anita. Yeah, I'll be by later to take a look at it."

He looked up as she limped to the corner of the sofa and leaned onto the padding of her crutches. "That was Anita at the sheriff's office. She called to let me know that they moved the major pieces of the helicopter to a different hangar." He waved the pad of paper. "Got the new address here, so we're set to go whenever we want to check it out."

He hopped to his feet, tucking his phone and notepad into his back pockets. "So, you ready to go?"

She led the way toward the door, showing him her keys before he could even ask. He waited for her on the second step as she locked the deadbolt behind them. As she turned toward him, he offered a hesitant smile.

She sighed, into her crutches, a pang of guilt knotting her stomach. "Sorry about before."

"Before?"

Was he really going to make her say it? The silence hanging in the air answered her unspoken question. "I'm really not a morning person, and I have a bit of a routine about my coffee and breakfast." She shrugged. "It's been a rough week. I already feel off balance."

"No worries. I get it." He tipped his head back toward the living room. "I'm sorry if I snored."

Then he reached out to her, as if to pick her up just

like the day before. For the second time that morning she shot him a glare that had crumbled weaker men.

"Or not." He laughed as he loped down the cement steps. "See you at the car…in fifteen minutes."

Why did this man insist on pushing every one of her buttons? How could she possibly put up with him for the rest of the investigation? She'd do it for Kit, of course. But that was the only thing that made her take measured steps after the infuriating man.

It took only about half the time Latham had suggested it would for Heather to make it down the stairs and get situated in the backseat of his cruiser.

Adjusting his rearview mirror, he asked, "All set?"

They made eye contact through the mirror, and she nodded as he pulled out of the space. As she passed her Saturn SUV, a little sigh escaped. It would be several weeks before the doctor released her to drive again. At least then she wouldn't be confined in this smelly cage.

"What do you think we're going to find at Kit's office?"

Truthfully she had no idea, even if she had been the one to convince him that it's where they needed to start. "I'm sure whatever Kit was looking into, she kept copious notes about it." She leaned over to readjust the angle of her knee. "That was just her style."

"I know."

"You do?" Her gaze shot to the mirror again, catching his for just a moment.

He shrugged, turning the sedan toward downtown Portland. A light mist covered the windshield, and his wipers reacted accordingly. "We met a few times."

Heather sat up straighter. "How? Did she prosecute a case you worked?"

"No. But she did for my friend Tony at the police department. Tony's the one who told me to get down to the morgue."

"I remember." Her voice was urgent, strained and unusual. She swallowed trying to get it back to normal.

"Tony and I were out celebrating closing a case one night, and we bumped into your sister. Tony introduced us, and I could see in her eyes that she wasn't missing a thing about me. I felt like she was going to start a file on me the minute she got back to her office. Maybe that's what we'll find today."

Heather chuckled. "That sounds just like her."

While they were stopped at a red light, she stared at the black hybrid next to them without really seeing it.

Jeremy had pegged Kit in a single meeting. She read people. She read situations, looking much deeper than the surface. So how had she not known that someone was after her, willing to take down the sightseeing helicopter?

Maybe she *had* known about them. But why keep it a secret, even from her own sister? Kit certainly hadn't told Clay, or he would have said something. Right?

The muscles in her neck tightened under the stress of this train of thought. As traffic moved again, she rubbed the nape of her neck and tilted her head up toward the fabric-covered ceiling.

God, I have to figure out who's responsible for Kit's death. I have to see... Don't you see that I have to see this through? Justice has to be served. What happened can't be for nothing. I just want justice.

Even in her mind, the prayer bounced off the felt, returning to her unanswered. The hollow words ricocheted around her head, only adding to the tension mounting there. Rubbing her temples didn't alleviate the pressure or change what had happened.

Had God really stopped listening to her prayers?

There was no time to dwell on the answer to that as Jeremy parked outside the large cement building. "Want the chair?" he asked before sliding from behind the wheel.

"No." She wrinkled her nose. "But I suppose I'd better."

Jeremy walked around the car, popping the trunk and closing it a few seconds later. "Who knows?" he said, as he opened the back door for her. "It might win us some sympathy points."

"Is that how you close cases in the sheriff's office, Deputy Latham? With sympathy points?"

He helped her settle into the hard leather seat and leaned toward her, resting both hands on the rigid armrests. "We do whatever it takes to get the case solved, Special Agent Sloan." His gaze hardened for a moment. "And this case is no exception. You can be sure that I'll do whatever it takes to figure out who brought that chopper down."

"Thank you."

Almost immediately he disappeared behind her, wheeling the chair between thick columns toward wooden doors.

After passing through security, each showing their badges and entering the elevator, Jeremy pushed the button for the third floor. "Have you been here before?" he asked.

"Just once, when she first started." Feeling compelled to explain why she'd only visited once in the four years her sister worked in the District Attorney's office, she continued. "We both had busy work lives and weren't actually in our offices that often. It was just easier to meet up for dinner after work or on weekends."

The elevator chimed, the doors opening on cue, and he pushed her over the one-inch step to the floor. They moved down the hallway, stopping at Room 600 just as a tall, thin woman in a severe suit opened the door. She held it open and nodded at Jeremy's quick thanks.

"Good morning." The receptionist was young, but her eagle eyes surveyed them. "Do you have an appointment?"

Heather shook her head. "No."

"Then, may I set one up for you? Our D.A.s are only available—"

Her words stopped at the instant that Heather held out her Bureau ID. Out of the corner of her eye, she could see that Jeremy had also pushed his jacket aside, showing his gold shield.

"This is Deputy Latham with the sheriff's department." Heather nodded in his direction. "And I'm Special Agent Heather Sloan."

The young woman's face crumbled before their eyes. "I'm sorry. I'm not supposed to let anyone in without an appointment." She swallowed loudly, reaching for the phone on her desk. Before she dialed, she looked back at Heather, brows pulled together. "Did you say Heather Sloan? As in…were you…did you know DDA Katherine Sloan?"

"She was my sister."

Heather hadn't ever seen anyone dial a phone as fast as the poor girl sitting in front of them. "Please, you have to come up here right now. No, now." She hung up, a sadness clearly spelled across her face.

Just when Heather was about to take pity on the girl and say something kind, another woman joined them.

Dark curls abused by the humidity and her face a mask of sorrow, she couldn't seem to take her eyes off of Heather.

"I'm Tonya Norton. I was Kit's assistant. Are you Heather?"

Now it was Heather's turn to be confused. "Have we met?"

"No. I don't think so. But Kit had a lot of pictures of the two of you up in her office. You look just like her. Just…"

"With a fair complexion," Heather supplied, offering her hand to the nodding woman. "It's good to meet you." She introduced Jeremy quickly. "He's investigating the helicopter crash, and we thought there might be some useful information in Kit's files."

"So, you think—" She broke off her words with a quick glance over her shoulder at the young receptionist suddenly making herself look busy. "Why don't I show you to Kit's office?"

Jeremy wheeled Heather down a short hallway and into what appeared to be just another vacant office. The large wooden desk was empty except for a white, file box with a plant and a few picture frames sticking over the edge.

Tonya closed the office door and pointed to a chair for Jeremy, then pulled out the one from behind the desk for herself. "This is a box of stuff that Kit had here in the office. I was going to contact you about picking it up."

"Thank you. I'll take it with me today." Heather poked around in it for a moment, hoping for files or anything useful. But it seemed to be only personal things.

Leaning toward them, Tonya whispered, "Do you

think it was foul play? Do you think someone purpose-fully sabotaged the helicopter?"

Heather looked to Jeremy, meeting his eyes imme-diately.

He cleared his throat. "We're investigating all the possibilities right now."

She leaned back, her tongue sucking on one of her back teeth. "Oh." Was that disappointment lacing Tonya's voice?

"Why?" Jeremy and Heather asked at the same time.

"Well, it's just that…maybe I shouldn't say anything. Maybe it was nothing."

Heather leaned onto her injured leg and groaned, quickly shifting to lean on her other elbow. "You can tell us anything. Let us decide if it's nothing."

Tonya's eyes shifted back and forth between the two sitting across from her. "I mean, I don't really know anything."

Jeremy bit the corner of his lower lip, leaning back from the revving emotions in the center of the room. "How long did you work with Ms. Sloan?"

"Three years. I've been with the office for more than seven, but when budgets were cut, we had to double up, assisting two of the D.D.A.s."

"Did you like working with my sister?"

Tonya's eyes turned watery. "Very much. She was so kind, always remembering my birthday or bringing me a latte for no reason." She brought her hands up to cover her face, revealing wrinkles and age spots that Heather hadn't noticed before.

Heather reached to pat the other woman's shoulder, but couldn't quite stretch that far from the wheelchair. She settled for a hum of understanding.

Jeremy continued questioning Tonya like she was a frail witness. "Had you noticed anything unusual about Kit's daily activities lately? Had she been late to work? Or had unusual visitors?"

"Oh, no. She was always very punctual. And she hadn't had any visitors lately except for her fiancé. He's very handsome." Out of the corner of her eye, Heather thought she saw Jeremy flinch, but she couldn't figure out why. "But…there was one thing."

"Mmm," Jeremy prodded.

Tonya's gaze darted around the room, as if confirming they were still alone. "I can't be sure exactly what it was, but a couple weeks ago I saw a file—like one of the case files—on her desk. She always had me start those, but this one didn't have a label on it, like I put on them."

"Could it have just been an empty folder on her desk?" Jeremy asked.

Shaking her head, Tonya said, "I don't think so. It wasn't new—one of the corners was bent—and it looked like it had several pieces of paper in it. Not full, really. But it wasn't empty."

Tonya's hands trembled, but Heather decided to press her just a bit more. "Did you ever see it again? That particular file or another one that didn't have one of your labels on it?"

"I'm pretty sure that she was reading the same one when I walked into her office to drop off some paperwork about two weeks ago."

"How do you know it was the same folder?"

"The corner was bent under in the same way, and it looked like it had about the same amount of paper in it."

Heather rubbed her hands over her face. How much

did Tonya really know about the situation? Was this folder really important or just a red herring to derail their investigation? Taking a deep breath through her nose and tucking her unruly curls behind her ears, she asked, "And what do you think this unlabeled folder means?"

It was Tonya's turn to rake her hands over her face. "I don't know."

Jeremy rolled his office chair closer to the older woman, invading her personal space just enough. Wrapping his large hand around the comparably birdlike structure of Tonya's forearm, he whispered, "Was it a case file? Did Kit start a file on a case and not tell you about it?"

Tears dribbled down her cheeks as she nodded. "I think so."

"What was she investigating?"

"I don't know."

"Where is that file now?"

More tears spilled down Tonya's face, and Heather's gut clenched. If the file had anything to do with Kit's death, they had to find out what was in it. It could solve the case and identify the person responsible for this nightmare so he could be punished.

Tonya swallowed loudly. "I don't know. When I cleaned out her office, I gave all the labeled files to the D.A., just like he told me to. And then I boxed up all of her personal items. I couldn't find that file anywhere."

Jeremy sat back, patting her shoulder with one hand. It looked like he nearly pulled his hair out by the roots with the other.

"Is that why?" Tonya's voice shook ever so slightly.

"Why what?" Heather asked.

"Is that missing file why Kit was killed?"

SIX

Jeremy shook Tonya's hand, balancing the box of Kit's personal belongings on the opposite arm and wishing he had an answer—any response—to the traumatized woman's question. "We'll be in touch soon. If you remember anything about that file, or anything else that seems unusual, please call me." He handed her his card as they walked toward the office of another D.D.A., one who Kit had worked with closely.

Just outside his door, Heather said, "Thank you for what you did. For being so good with Tonya in there."

What was he doing besides his job? If she thought he was giving special preference to the case and possible witnesses, she was wrong. Sure, he was staying with his only true witness to the crash. But that was for her own protection and his benefit. She couldn't help him find the culprit if she was taken out of the picture.

Beyond that, this case was just that—another case.

But if that was true, why did every part of this assignment remind him of the greatest failure of his career? One that had cost four of his friends, including his fiancée, their lives.

He wasn't getting emotionally involved in solving this crash. He wouldn't. He would simply work the case, solve the crime. And keep Heather safe while he was at it. It had no link to his past mistakes. It couldn't, because he couldn't handle going through something like that again.

"You ready, Latham?" Heather's eyes asked a deeper question. Was his head in the game? Because she needed it to be.

Okay, maybe his heart was a little bit invested. But maybe if he could help Heather find justice in the midst of her loss, he could find some resolution—some absolution—for his sins. He could never undo the mistake he made or bring back Reena, but there might be some peace for him when Heather's heart could begin to heal.

He nodded firmly. "Yes. Let's go." He tipped his head toward Tonya in thanks before rapping on the glass door with his knuckle. Pushing it open just a bit, he poked his head around the pane. "Mr. Smithers?"

A skinny man with tiny glasses perched on his overly large nose looked up from his computer screen. "May I help you?"

Jeremy pulled back his jacket to show off his badge. "I'm Deputy Jeremy Latham with the Multnomah County Sheriff's Department."

Smithers' eyes brightened. "Of course. I tried one of your cases last year. It was pretty open and shut, if I recall."

"That's right."

"What can I do for you?"

Jeremy pushed the door open a little farther, and Heather wheeled herself into the gap between him and the door frame. "This is Special Agent Heather Sloan."

Smithers' face immediately fell. "Kit's sister?"

"Yes," she confirmed.

Smithers looked like a beanpole as he stood and walked around his desk, coming to meet both of them but holding his hand out only to Heather. "I am so sorry for your loss. Kit was a very special woman."

Heather quickly agreed, and Jeremy couldn't help but wonder if Kit was really as wonderful as everyone said. Could anyone be so kind and perfect? Or was that just what everyone wanted to remember? Maybe she really was just like Mary Poppins. Or maybe she was mixed up in something that got her killed and nearly took her sister's life as well.

For Heather's sake he was willing to believe the best of Kit. Unless they found proof otherwise.

"How closely did you work with Kit?" Heather asked the other man, who leaned against his desk.

"Well, we shared an assistant. And sometimes we'd consult on cases together, but we didn't spend that much time together in or out of the office."

"Would you call her a friend?" Jeremy said.

Smithers rubbed the tip of his nose and blinked in rapid succession. "She was great, and I enjoyed working with her. But we weren't that close. She was more of a professional acquaintance."

"You said that you sometimes consulted on cases together," Heather said.

"Sure."

"What was the last case that you discussed?"

Again Smithers blinked six times in a row, and Jeremy had a sudden urge to find the man a bottle of eye drops. "I'm afraid it's still an active case. I can't discuss it with anyone outside this office except for the arresting officer."

"Can we speak in generalities, then?" The other man

nodded, and Jeremy continued. "Did Kit consult with you about any cases involving illegal street drugs? Either a case you were taking to trial or one she was?"

Smithers' eyes rolled toward the ceiling as his forehead wrinkled. "The last drug case we talked about was almost a year ago, and it was my case. Kit was usually assigned to felony cases more likely to go to trial because she was so good in the courtroom. A lot of the drug cases we get end up in plea bargains, so the D.A. usually didn't assign those cases to Kit." He blinked again, and tugged on the hair at his temple. "Why? Do you think Kit's death was a result of criminal activity?"

Jeremy glanced toward Heather, who maintained eye contact with Smithers. Her slender hands trembled for just a second, but she clamped them together before the thin man seemed to notice. Undoubtedly she could handle answering the question, but Jeremy had a sudden urge to save her from having to respond about her sister.

"We're exploring all possibilities."

Smithers' gaze moved back to Jeremy. "If there's anything I can do to help, please let me know. We might not have been good friends, but I liked and respected Kit. She was a good attorney, and we certainly miss her."

"Thank you," Heather and Jeremy said at the same time. He shot her a quick grin, as he collected the box of Kit's personal belongings.

They offered a quick farewell to Tonya as they passed her desk on the way out of the office, but other than that, they were both silent as they headed toward the elevator and back to the first floor. Heather held the box on her lap as he pushed her across the street to his car.

Pressing the brakes on the wheels, Jeremy took the

box, sliding it all the way across the backseat. When he turned back to Heather, she had almost pushed herself all the way to a standing position. But he clumsily bumped her arm, and she began to sway on one foot, her face turning into a mask of fear and humiliation.

Without thought, he reached for her, his hands wrapping around her waist and pulling her close enough that he could smell the coconut shampoo she'd used that morning. "I'm sorry. I wasn't trying to knock you over."

Her hands latched on to his arms just below the shoulders, as she chuckled. "Don't think you're getting rid of me that easily. We have an agreement."

He tugged her a fraction of an inch closer until her good knee bumped against his, and he realized in that moment that he had absolutely no desire to get rid of her. And it had very little to do with their agreement and almost everything to do with the way that she made him laugh and the way his stomach twisted in a knot and his heart beat a little harder just standing next to her.

She was beautiful and spunky and guaranteed to complicate his life.

It was better that their partnership was based only on their agreement to solve this case. Pushing any wayward emotions aside he nearly lifted her off her feet placing her in the backseat. "Yes, we do."

Heather stared at the back of Jeremy's head as he maneuvered the car back into traffic. She'd been certain that she was going to hit the ground when he bumped into her a moment ago. The brace surrounding her leg, even over her jeans, looked like a brick, holding her back, keeping her from doing what it would take to solve this case. She wanted to hit the ugly brackets with her fist, but she'd done that once before by accident. It hurt worse than she thought it should have.

But maybe her frustration had more to do with the way her skin reacted to being so close to him than her own limitations.

She could still feel his arms around her waist and the way his proximity made goose bumps erupt up and down her arms. He was strong, but not like he spent every day in the gym. It was muscle from hard work, training for his job. Like maybe he chopped firewood on the weekends for the fun of it.

That thought made her nearly laugh out loud at its absurdity. Until she remembered the up-close view of his five-o'clock shadow, which had already started to darken his perfect jawline, and the roguish grin that had crossed his face.

Any other time, any other reason for knowing him, and she probably would have appreciated his handsome face and teasing humor. But not now. Not with Kit's memory so fresh.

"So?" Jeremy's single syllable yanked her mind back to her surroundings.

"What?" She caught his eye in the mirror, and he looked to the right, his eyebrows jumping slightly. She just shook her head, confused.

"The box. Are you going to look in it?"

Maybe her leg injury was affecting more than her ability to stand up without falling over. She should have thought to open the box immediately. "Of course. Yes." She hoped he couldn't see the heat tinting her cheeks as she pulled the white file box toward her, resting it on the seat next to her leg brace.

She set the cardboard lid to the side, pulling out a picture of her and Kit as kids, standing in their parents' front yard, arms draped across the other's shoulder. Heather hadn't seen the picture in ages. The ornate silver frame had been a birthday gift from Heather to her sister years before, but Heather thought the last time she had seen it, there might have been another picture in it.

Setting the picture on top of the box lid, she pulled out a small potted plant and from habit checked it for bugs. Both the biological and technological kinds.

"Is it clean?" Jeremy asked.

"Yes."

Next came a folder, like the one that Tonya had described. Except that this one had been clearly labeled Kit's Personal Items.

"There's a folder in here. It's labeled, but maybe there's something of use to us in it," Heather said. Jeremy nodded as he turned a sharp corner. Leaning even more heavily against the door, she flipped through the pages. "Her cell phone bill. Electric. Receipts for some work on her car." Snapping the edges of the folder closed, she sighed. "Nothing else in here."

"Anything else in the box that might be of use?"

She sifted through the few other pictures, a law book, an engraved fountain pen and Kit's wooden name plate.

"Not a single thing that's useful. It's all just stuff that you'd find on anyone's desk." Only knowing the ache it would cause kept her from hitting her head against the window. "I'm sorry. I guess we should've gone to check out the wreckage first."

"Don't worry about it. We'll find the information we need."

"I know we will. But today was a complete waste. Now our guy is one more day ahead of us."

He waited until she looked at him in the rearview

mirror. "No, it wasn't a waste." She tried to interrupt him, but he shot her a stern glare. "Now we know that Kit was looking into something that she wasn't sharing with anyone else at work. And it might be related to the drugs she warned you about."

"Yes, but we have no idea what it was."

He smiled. "But we can figure that out. Before we went to her office, we didn't even know for sure that we should be looking for something she was investigating. Now we do."

He was right. She knew he was. But she just couldn't admit it.

She groaned, pushing her hair off her face and tucking a curl behind her ear. "You didn't even want to go to her office today."

His laugh was quiet and assured, completely free from embarrassment. "Guilty as charged. But it doesn't mean that I don't know a good investigative tactic when I see one. You're pretty good at this."

The offhanded compliment made her smile, despite the yawn that suddenly cracked her jaw. "Imagine how much better I'd have been today if I'd had my mug and drinkable coffee."

This time his laugh was deep, rumbling right along with the engine. "And you're funny, too. Is there anything you can't do, Special Agent Sloan?"

"Nope." Covering another yawn with the back of her hand, she battled the fog that reminded her of her time in the hospital. It wasn't even noon yet, but the supposedly nondrowsy painkillers prescribed by the doctor at the hospital had kicked in. She'd had her doubts about the "nondrowsy" part, and sure enough they made her want to curl up and take a long nap.

Fighting that urge, she asked, "What next? Should we go to the hangar to see the wreckage?"

"Sounds like a plan." Jeremy pulled a U-turn at the next stoplight, and they sailed toward the hangar where agents of both the FAA and the sheriff's department inspected the remains of the helicopter.

They were silent for a long while as he expertly navigated the Portland streets. He appeared deep in thought, and Heather wasn't interested in starting a conversation just to pass the time. But she couldn't help but wonder what they might find when they saw the twisted metal and shattered glass that could easily have taken her life, too. "Did Anita say anything else on the phone this morning—other than the location of the new hangar?"

"Nope. I'm sure they're still analyzing what's left of the chopper to confirm the cause of the crash. When I worked for the FAA, we could usually nail down the reason behind a crash long before we could give the official word on it."

"Wait. You worked for the FAA?"

He turned the car down onto a long street lined with industrial warehouses, many red with rust and looking like a sturdy rain would level them. "It was a while ago."

She waited for him to expound, but the tight clench of his jaw didn't look as if it was going to relax at any point. "So then, how did you end up at the sheriff's department?"

He didn't respond, only turned onto a gravel street that crunched under the tires and stones went flying when he stomped on the brakes in front of a relatively sturdy metal warehouse. It appeared just as beaten by the elements as the structures on either side of it, but it seemed to stand a little straighter, a little stronger than its neighbors.

Jeremy helped her out of the car and into the wheelchair, the lines of his cheeks still tense as she offered him an apologetic smile.

He still didn't speak as he pushed the chair through the bed of rocks toward a small unmarked door near the left corner of the building. When they reached it, he pulled out his phone and punched one key. "We're here."

Several seconds later, the door hummed low, and he pushed it open with his back, wheeling Heather in backward. Immediately she began blinking, trying to adjust to the lights that illuminated rows of long tables.

On the far side of the room, the skeleton of the wrecked chopper sat. Dents and scratches from the crash marred the white and blue exterior.

"Latham, good to see you, man." A middle-aged man with a receding hairline and large girth pumped Jeremy's hand, while never taking his eyes off Heather.

The hair on her arms stood up, and if she had been mobile on her own, she would have slid a little closer to Jeremy. As it was, she leaned heavily on the armrest closest to him, keeping a wary eye on the older man.

"Udahl." Jeremy's voice didn't indicate any of the pleasure in the other man's tone. "It's been awhile."

"Sure has. Who's your friend?"

Jeremy's gaze darted in Heather's direction, and he took a minuscule step in front of her, blocking her from Udahl's view. "We're working a case together." He nodded toward the tables. "This one. What do you have?"

Just then a woman, at least a couple years younger than Heather, trotted up to them. She grabbed Heather's hand right out of her lap. "You must be Heather. I'm Anita. Anita Brigget. I'm so glad to meet you." Heather just nodded as the other woman babbled along. "Jeremy said you'd be coming with him, and I was just so eager to meet you. He said you're working the case together. What do you do?"

Jeremy cut in, shooting Heather a pointed stare. "She's working the case with me."

Anita's forehead wrinkled as she looked back and forth between them, but she was undeterred. "So you met Agent Udahl."

"Agent?" Heather swallowed the sudden urge to cough as the smarmy man rubbed his hands together. No way was he with the Bureau. Of course, she'd know him if he were in the Portland office. But even if he was from another office, he could rat her out to Nate.

"With the FAA."

The breath she'd been holding let loose, but she still didn't smile at him.

"All right," Jeremy interrupted. "We're all introduced. What have you got for us?"

Udahl puckered his lips to the left and wrinkled his nose as though debating if he was ready to move on. Thankfully Anita had no such qualms, and immediately walked toward the nearest table, where pieces of metal and plastic lay across the entire table. Next to each piece from the wreck rested a tag identifying what part of the aircraft it came from. A group of lab techs in white coats continued the identification process at another table across the hangar.

Snapping on a pair of rubber gloves, Anita picked up the black metal joystick. Turning it over gently, she lifted several wires at its base.

Jeremy immediately leaned in. "Those were cut."

"Yes, but not all the way." Anita turned them over. "See here? This edge is frayed."

Jeremy caught Heather's gaze and grimaced. "So someone severed the controls to the cyclic. They left just enough control to get the chopper back in the air, and then the wires would have frayed the rest of the way."

Udahl nodded. "It had to have been done when the pilot stopped to refuel. Would have taken less than ten minutes for someone to get in there and get it done."

Heather rubbed her throat and chest, fighting the pain building there. How could someone be so cruel? She pressed her lips together, biting down to keep from saying anything that would force her to relive the terror of the crash.

"Did you find anything else?"

"Like what?" Anita asked.

Jeremy shrugged. "Anything unusual. Out of the ordinary. Criminal."

"No. Not yet, at least. Why?"

He lifted one shoulder again. "Just curious. Will you let me know if you do?"

"Of course."

"Great. Then we'll let you get back to work."

"Drop by anytime," Udahl said, his eyes again roaming over Heather's seated form.

She shuddered as Jeremy pushed her toward the door, and she mumbled, "Not likely."

Back on the road, she couldn't contain another jaw-cracking yawn. It was the middle of the afternoon, and even though they'd skipped lunch, what she really wanted was a nap.

"It seems very strange." Jeremy seemed to be talking to himself.

"What's that?"

"I guess I just figured there would be something on the helicopter that would point to something criminal, to a reason to bring it down." He stared straight ahead, and she could still see his jaw clenching and unclenching as he worked out his thoughts.

"Maybe they just haven't gotten to it. It's only been nine days since the crash."

"Maybe."

Heather could tell he wasn't convinced. "Or maybe it's at the crash site."

His head snapped up at that, and he nodded slowly. "Of course."

"Should we head over there and see if they left anything behind by accident?"

"Let's wait until tomorrow. By the time we'd get out there today, it'd only be light for an hour or so." He braked as the light in front of them turned yellow, and peeked at her over his right shoulder. "You look beat. Why don't you get some rest this afternoon while I do some paperwork?"

"I told you that I wouldn't slow you down, and I'm not tired," she fibbed, a little bit of her hoping that he'd insist anyway.

"Well, I really do need to stop by the office and check in. I'll drop you off at your place, and then I'll be back in just a little while."

With a silent sigh, she sank lower into the door against her back. Why did she still have to feel so weak after the crash? She hadn't needed a nap since she was six, but now tremors in her hands signaled that something was definitely off. Lack of sleep was probably the least of her concerns, but all she really cared about was seeing the person responsible for Kit's death punished. Justice had to be done.

Swiftly.

SEVEN

"How was your physical therapy this morning?"

Heather looked up from her favorite mug filled with what she called "not just drinkable coffee, but coffee that actually tastes good." Her shoulders relaxed as she leaned into the back of the kitchen chair. "Good. The knee is still a little stiff, but I'm doing the exercises just like the therapist said."

"How long until you can sit in the front seat of the car?" Jeremy couldn't help the grin tugging at the corner of his mouth, so he covered it by turning back to the sink, washing his own coffee mug. He could practically hear her scowl as the legs of her chair scraped along the tile.

"Soon. Very soon." Balanced on one leg, she set her mug on the counter, and he scooped it into the hot sudsy water.

Her crutches clattered together, and he snuck a glance over his shoulder to make sure she didn't need an extra hand as she headed toward the front door. With even strides she lumbered across the living room until she turned, looking at him expectantly.

"You about ready?"

The water swished down the drain with a loud slurp.

Wiping his hands on the legs of his jeans and then grabbing his keys off the table, he jogged toward her. "All set."

Her movements down the steps were still awkward, but she had picked up some speed in the course of just a couple days. And today she didn't even need help getting into the back of the car. She'd figured out how to slide in without jarring her leg. All he did was hold her crutches and then slide them onto the floorboard when she was situated.

The gentle rumble of the engine reigned as the car headed southeast along Highway 26 toward the scene of the helicopter crash. At length Jeremy broke the silence.

"Did you get a chance to look through the things from Kit's office again yesterday afternoon?" When he'd left her at her house, she had been nearly sleepwalking from exhaustion. And when he'd returned more than two hours later, she'd been passed out in the living room chair, snoring softly, mouth hanging open.

"No, I... Well, I fell asleep in the chair. I think the painkillers I'm taking for my leg are making me sleepy."

"Mmm." By sheer will, he kept his mouth closed. They both knew the truth. Investigating any crime was tiring on the best day. Throw in recovering from injuries from the crash, a major surgery and the emotional tumult of losing her sister, and Heather had to be drained.

He made a mental note to be sure he got her back to her house for regular naps and full nights of sleep. If this one was anything like other drug cases he'd worked, it would likely get sticky before it got better. And they both needed to be alert and ready for whatever was coming their way.

Suddenly Heather chuckled, and it sounded like it was right beside his ear. "Okay. I confess. I was just so tired. I couldn't keep my eyes open." Her cheeks turned a very attractive shade of pink. Apparently she could make fun of herself. "I don't think it was the medication."

He shot her a smile in return. She needed more rest. Recovery from injuries like hers wasn't going to be a breeze. He needed to make sure she got just what she required. And maybe a cup of his mom's chicken noodle soup. "It's okay. We'll go back through the box again another day."

"But I don't think there's anything in there that'll be of use to us," she said. "It's just all so ordinary."

"Okay. So what *do* we know? About the case. And about your sister."

She exhaled loudly and stared at the ceiling for several long seconds. "We know that Kit thought that something or someone having to do with drugs was behind the crash." In his mirror, she licked her lips, eyes squinting out the far window.

"What's on your mind?"

"I'm just wondering who cut those wires in the…"

"The cyclic."

"Yes." Worrying the corner of her lower lip, she stared through the windshield into the sparse forest spread out before them like a blanket of green and brown. "It happened just like you said—the fraying giving way and leaving us with no control while we were midair. The pilot said it wasn't working. He jerked it around, but nothing stopped us from going down."

They both mulled over the information at hand for several seconds before Heather veered down a different path. "Why didn't you tell me you had been with the FAA?"

"I did. I told you yesterday."

"Yes, but you haven't said two words about it since. Why did you leave? Why join the sheriff's office?"

Jeremy spotted a dirt road just ahead off to the left of the highway. Slowing down, he pulled the car off the pavement as they bounced over the ruts and roots. Large pine trees shaded them from the unusually bright sun.

Heather looked like she still expected an answer to her question, but he had no desire to rehash his history. If he told her about his time with the FAA, inevitably he'd have to tell her why he left and moved nearly three thousand miles across the country to work as a sheriff's deputy. And then he'd have to explain about Reena.

About faulty gauge upgrades on a Cessna 172 Skyhawk that he should have checked.

About watching his fiancée and three friends die in a crash he could have prevented.

He'd much rather just work on the case at hand and put the past to rest, letting Heather begin her own healing. Moving forward here was better than looking back on mistakes that still haunted his dreams.

A tree appeared in the middle of his barely-there road, which had only been used by the ambulance and service personnel, and he swerved sharply. Heather thudded against the back of his seat, groaning. "Sorry. Are you hurt?"

"No. I'm fine." Her hands dug into his back, even through the upholstered seat, as she pushed herself back into a comfortable spot. "Is that it?" she suddenly asked, her neck craning out the side window.

The scar in the trees appeared to their left, broken limbs and dead pine needles marking the ill-fated path of the helicopter. Several pine trees looked as though they'd taken quite a beating from the rotor but had remained whole. As Jeremy pulled the car closer to the clearing where the chopper had finally come to a stop, he spotted a young pine that had been snapped in half near the tail of the aircraft.

"This is it," he finally responded to Heather.

"It sure didn't look like this the last time I saw it."

He pulled to a stop about a hundred feet from the clearing and slipped out from behind the steering wheel, closing his door before opening hers. He slipped on a bed of needles and stubbed his toe on a hidden rock, as he took the last step toward her. "I don't think the chair is going to cut it here. I won't be able to get you over these fallen branches, and the pine needles mean there'd be no traction for the wheels."

"That's fine. I'll be okay." She reached for her crutches, but he cleared his throat.

"Why don't we just stick together? You can lean on me, because those crutches aren't going to be much use to you either. It's too slippery out here." He glanced toward the gray skies out of habit, wondering when the next storm would rip through the area.

She hesitated for a moment.

"What's wrong?"

Heather twisted her neck and squinted up into Jeremy's face. Did he seriously think she was going to let him carry her around the crash site?

Probably.

His eyes turned stubborn, like she knew her own were.

"Well, you can either let me help you, or you can stay in the car." His hands rested loosely on his hips, the relaxed pose contradicting the note in his voice that said he wasn't going to give way on this.

She sighed in resignation and reached her hand back toward him. He ducked under it, wrapping his arm around her waist and tucking her against his side. In an instant she stood balanced precariously on her good leg, leaning heavily into him. His breath tickled the back of her neck through her hair, and her stomach took a nosedive into her tennis shoes. He smelled fresh and clean, adding nothing to the forest air except the warmth of his body.

She wanted to sink back into that warmth. Wanted to forget why they were there, why they'd had to pair up. She just wanted to enjoy the way the butterflies in her stomach jumped to life when he held her close.

Glancing up into his face, she wondered from the tight pull of his lips and glint in his dark eyes if he felt the same things she did.

But she had to keep her mind on why they were stuck together.

Justice had to be served, and she hoped she'd get to be there when the man, who cut those wires, got what he deserved.

It wasn't until Jeremy winked at her that she realized she'd been staring into his eyes for who knew how long.

"Come on," he said, tugging his arm tighter around her waist.

She didn't have much of a choice, so she hobbled along beside him, her hand resting on the muscles of his shoulder that bunched every time she took a step.

"Would it be easier if I carried you?"

"No."

He chuckled. "I didn't think so." As they stepped

into the clearing, he asked, "Do you remember anything from that day? I mean, except what Kit said?"

"Not really." Why wouldn't her brain let her remember anything useful? When she closed her eyes and tried to focus on the crash, all she could see was the pain in Kit's face. And Kit breathing those last words. *Follow the drugs.*

"It was so loud. Not just the helicopter, but the sound of the trees crunching and metal being ripped away." She pulled herself up on his arm as she hopped over a fallen branch, her eyes sweeping the ground where her foot landed for anything out of the ordinary.

Jeremy led them on a slow walk around the perimeter of the clearing, kicking at small piles of leaves. "The sheriff's department didn't find anything except those cut wires that pointed to foul play when they picked up the pieces of wreckage. But it's rained a couple times since the crash."

"So anything left from the crash will have been washed away. Except what's been protected by the trees."

He squeezed her waist. "You're pretty good at this, you know?"

"That's the second time you've complimented me on my investigating skills. Keep it up, and I'll start to think you're not working with me under duress."

Silent humor jostled her hand on his shoulder, as something metallic glinted in the bit of sun revealed by a passing cloud. "What's that?" She pointed, urging him on.

When they reached the glimmer of silver, Heather leaned on a tree, as he dropped to a knee, pushing mud and pinecones out of the way to reveal a soda can. Holding it up for her inspection, he asked, "Did you have anything to drink on the ride up to Mount St. Helens?"

"Kit and I shared a bottle of water. But that's it."

"What about the pilot?"

"I don't think he had anything."

He crushed the can with one hand and pocketed it before resuming their stroll beneath the trees. Twenty minutes later and just over halfway around the clearing, Heather saw something else, but it, too, was just a piece of litter.

And it wasn't until they stopped the second time that she realized her hands were shaking. Her thigh burning from exerting it more than she'd done since the crash, she leaned heavily onto the tree. Her head began spinning, and she pressed the heels of her palms into her eyes to battle the black spots suddenly dancing there.

When Jeremy reached out for her, she put her hand into his, and stumbled against his chest.

"Whoa." He ducked his head to look into her eyes, using his right thumb to dab a bead of sweat from her temple. "Are you all right?"

"Yes. Of course. I'm fine." She blinked three times and swallowed something that tasted suspiciously like defeat.

He shook his head. "I'm pushing you too hard. You've barely been out of bed four days, and I'm dragging you around all of northwest Oregon."

"No! I'm fine." She swiped at the line of sweat suddenly forming on her upper lip with the back of her hand. "We can keep going."

"You're a bad liar," he mumbled, as he turned to fit her back into his side. "I'm taking you back to the car."

She sucked in a quick breath, and exhaled. "I'm fine."

Chastising herself for the weakness in her voice, she tried again, this time looking right into his eyes. "I'm okay. I just need a little rest."

He sighed. "I think I have some water in the car." He nodded toward the least mossy boulder beneath a tree. "You take a seat, and I'll go get it."

She nodded, lowering herself onto the bleached rock, her braced leg stretched in front of her at an odd angle, hands propped next to her thighs to keep from leaning too far in any direction. Jeremy jogged straight to the car and disappeared into the passenger side, emerging several seconds later with a refillable water bottle.

The sweat that had appeared on her face was slowly disappearing, and her head began clearing.

"How're you feeling?" he said, when he returned to her.

"Like an idiot."

"Don't. We just have to remember that you're not quite back up to speed yet." He held the blue bottle toward her.

She studied his face as she reached for the bottle, looking for signs he might change his mind about working with her on the case. Suddenly a muscle in his jaw jumped, and he yanked the water back, grabbing her wrist with the opposite hand and turning her palm faceup. "What is that?"

Heather jerked her hand back, analyzing the white film covering most of her palm. "I don't know what it is," she said, gingerly touching it with the finger of her other hand. The residue clung to her finger, leaving a small circle of flesh surrounded by powder on her open palm.

Jeremy tucked the water bottle under his arm and reached for her hand again, turning it in the muted sunlight. His lips pursed as he leaned toward it, inhaling deeply.

A fine mist rose from her hand, and he jumped back before it could touch his nose.

She surveyed her other hand, which was completely free of the white powder. A large stain covered only the right side of the boulder, barely visible against the washed-out color of the rock. She leaned away from it to see if she'd sat in it. The residue stopped a fraction of an inch from where her thigh had been.

With a sure grip on her arm, Jeremy pulled her to her feet and into his side, wrapping an arm around her waist to stabilize her.

"Are you thinking what I'm thinking?" he finally asked. Her heart thudded painfully, the beating echoing in her ears.

"Cocaine?"

EIGHT

"Yes. You have much experience with the stuff?"

She shook her head. "I helped out on a drug case last year, but it was more money laundering than drugs."

"Do you have your footing?"

Her mind couldn't follow his train of thought as it changed tracks, and all she could offer in response was, "Huh?"

Loosening his grip around her middle, he stepped closer to the rock, keeping his eyes locked on hers. "You're not going to fall over if I let go?"

"No."

"Good," he said, reaching into his pocket and pulling out a little yellow evidence envelope. Bending the edge of the envelope, he scraped a bit of the cocaine onto the lip, then closed and sealed it. "Let's get this back to the lab." He waved the packet toward the car.

Heather dug into the pocket of her jeans, pulling out her cell phone. "First, we take a few pictures." Snapping a few close-ups of the white stain on the boulder and shots of the larger scene, she took an innocent step backward. Her leg crumbled like a sand castle under the force of a wave, pain shooting to her knee.

In a split second she knew she'd be on the ground,

but there was nothing to do. Until a strong arm wrapped around the middle of her back and another looped under her thighs, lifting her high against a broad chest. Out of instinct she grabbed his shoulders, her face inches from his. His breath stirred her hair, and the tightness around his lips confessed that he was fighting a smile.

"Let's get you back home."

The hammering of her heart nearly drowned out his words, but she shook her head out of habit. Whatever he wanted, she was nearly certain she wanted the opposite.

He started walking through the middle of the clearing, still carrying her.

"Put me down. I can walk."

"Like you did a minute ago? No, thanks. Picking you up once today is enough."

She huffed and would have crossed her arms, except for the disobedient limb slung around his neck that just wouldn't let go.

Jeremy had a sneaking suspicion that the pink in Heather's cheeks wasn't just from overexertion, but he forced his gaze away from the neat line of freckles parading over the bridge of her nose. Surveying the ground and rocks in the nearby area for any other sign of drugs, he pushed away the desire to focus on Heather's arm around his neck, which flexed every time he stepped over a fallen branch or rock.

"Are you worried I'm going to drop you?"

She shook her head. "No. Why?"

"You're hanging on awfully tight."

"I am?" She squinted up toward him, eyes bashful but still not loosening her clasp.

The sudden urge to hold her tighter and a lot longer

than necessary kicked him in the pit of his stomach, but he kept his grip steady. After all, the last woman he'd held tightly, he'd put on a plane that he'd watched crash. A fleeting desire to be close to this woman wasn't worth the heartache that would inevitably come if he failed to protect her.

As he stopped at the rear door of his car, he bent his knees and gently dropped Heather's feet to the ground. Dry pine needles crunched under foot, and her hands flew to grasp the roof of the car for stability.

Apparently she didn't want to hold on to him any longer than she had to.

He barely touched her as she slipped back into her seat, pulling the door closed behind her.

Just focus on the drugs, Latham. Get the case solved, and then this girl will be safe and out of your life. Things will go back to the way they were. That's what you want, right?

Of course. What else would he want?

Behind the wheel and back on the bumpy dirt road, Jeremy glanced over his shoulder. Heather seemed to be staring straight through the trees, little lines puckering the corners of her eyes.

"What are you thinking about?"

Her voice was softer than he'd ever heard it. "Kit was right about the drugs."

"I know."

"She must have been terrified." Another glance revealed that her gaze hadn't turned toward him. "What did she know about these drugs that kept her from telling me until the very last moment?"

Jeremy shrugged. "I don't know. Do you think she knew they were on board the helicopter?"

"I can't believe she would have. She was a deputy

D.A. There's no way she would have gone on that trip knowing what it was carrying. I sure wouldn't have."

"Then who did?"

Heather shook her head, her chin falling toward her chest and eyes closing. "The pilot?"

"Maybe. But if whoever knew about the drugs also cut those wires, the pilot isn't a good suspect." He cleared his throat as he pulled back onto the paved highway. "Unless it was some kind of suicide mission."

Heather looked up toward the roof, her nose wrinkling. "No way. He was scared." In the rearview mirror her hands came together in front of her, as though wrapping around the helicopter's controller. "He was genuinely afraid, yanking on the joystick and yelling at us to make sure we were buckled in. If it was a kamikaze mission, I think he would have just taken us down. He fought to keep us airborne."

"Good point. Okay, so if the pilot knew about the drugs, he certainly didn't know about the plan to bring the chopper down." As Jeremy slowed for a chipmunk to scurry across the road, he asked, "Who does that leave?"

"PNW Sightseeing?"

"The company that owns the aircraft?"

"Sure. Why not?"

Jeremy shook his head. "I think the better question is, why? Why would a smallish air tour company destroy one of its helicopters and kill a pilot and passenger?"

The corners of Heather's lips turned down, and she turned to look out the window again. "I don't know." She sighed, her shoulders slumping. He could read the discouragement on her face as clearly as he did the morning paper.

"Maybe we don't have to answer the 'why' question

right now." She perked up a bit, nodding slowly, as though thinking exactly the same thought.

"Maybe the real question we have to answer right now is simpler. Who had access to the helicopter?"

He caught her eye and gave her a grin. "I was thinking the same thing." Her smile matched his, as she leaned her head against the back of the seat. Sometimes having answers at that exact moment wasn't as important as knowing they were headed in the right direction.

"Let's drop this sample off at the lab along with your pictures," he said.

"And then let's pay a visit to our friends at PNW."

Heather had decided to wait in the car while Jeremy took the sample and her phone into the crime lab so the techs could download her pictures. They agreed that it would make their trip twice as long and only delay getting to PNW if she accompanied him inside.

She hadn't admitted to him that exhaustion played a role in her easy agreement to stay behind as well, but she had a sneaking suspicion that he knew that, too.

A shallow breeze came through the partially opened window, and she leaned against the seat, closing her eyes for just a moment. Sleep tugged at her mind, and she wanted to succumb, if just for a short nap. But something pinched the back of her brain, refusing to turn her thoughts off. Whatever it was, it kept bouncing around, telling her that she'd left something undone.

Had she left the stove on? Or forgot to unplug her hair dryer?

Doubtful.

So what made her stomach clench in uncertainty?

Jeremy yanked open the door, plopping down behind the wheel and tossing her phone to her. "I've been thinking," he said without even putting the key in the ignition.

"Me, too."

"What are you thinking?" he asked, turning to look her directly in the eye. His tone was serious, any indication of his usual humor gone.

"I'm not sure. It just feels like we're not asking all of the right questions." She pinched the arch of her nose in an attempt to relieve some of the pressure building there. "Like why were there even drugs on the helicopter?"

"Exactly what I was thinking." He rested his arm on the back of the front seat, the sleeve of his T-shirt snug against his biceps. She kicked herself for letting her mind focus on that fact, if even for a moment. It wasn't helping the case. "If the person who sabotaged the helicopter was behind the drugs and knew they were there, why would he destroy them in the crash?"

"This doesn't make any sense!" Heather barely kept from kicking the seat in front of her in frustration. "Kit knew there were drugs involved. But she couldn't have known they were on the helicopter."

"Wait. Let's back up for a second. Why would someone have cocaine on a chopper?"

"They're either hiding it or transporting it."

He nodded. "Right. Did you make any stops on the trip?"

Heather's stomach sank. "Just that one fuel stop on the other side of the Washington state line, on the way back. We weren't supposed to have one, but the pilot said our flight had taken longer than expected." She sucked on one of her fingernails, chewing but not biting it off. "Do you think he picked up a package?"

"Did you see anything?"

"Kit and I both went inside to use the restroom.

I didn't see anything, but that doesn't mean nothing happened."

Jeremy nodded slowly. "I can't see why you would have had to stop. The tank on the recovered aircraft had only a few gallons of fuel. It would have just made it back to the hangar. If the pilot was so concerned about making it back safely, he would have given himself a little bit of leeway. It just doesn't make sense that he would have stopped for barely enough to get you back."

"I guess we'd better talk to his coworkers and see what's going on at PNW."

He turned around, a focused look still on his face, and started the car. The pair remained silent for the entire twenty-minute drive to the PNW sightseeing offices.

At one point Heather opened her mouth to ask Jeremy if he was as confused by this scenario as she was, but the fear that he would find her skills lacking made her bite her tongue. Instead she rolled the questions around in her mind until she thought she might go crazy. None of it made sense. If the person responsible for the crash was also behind the drugs, why would he knowingly risk thousands of dollars worth of merchandise?

The answers didn't come easily, and soon they pulled up to an oversize metal shed, the letters PNW stenciled in black paint against the gray wall. Jeremy pulled around the gravel lot and stopped a few yards from the front door.

A cardboard clock with red arms claimed that the office was closed for another half hour, but the door was ajar.

"Worth a shot?" he said.

"Let's go." He scooted from behind the steering wheel, and as he walked past her window, she tapped on the glass and shook her head. He opened the back door for her, one eyebrow arched. "I'll use the crutches this time." She handed them out to him, and he held them with one hand, helping her out of the car with the other.

"Feeling steady?" he asked after she had the crutches in position. Her injured leg throbbed, reminding her that she had already used it more than she should have for the day. She nodded anyway, letting him lead the way.

The crunch of gravel under the rubber tips seemed excessively loud when the only other noise came from chirping birds. She tried to keep her movements light and silent, but even when they reached the cement sidewalk, the crutches clicked and clacked.

At the front door, Jeremy pulled on the handle, and it swung out with a loud creak. No use trying to be subtle about their entrance, so he called, "Hello! Anyone here? Multnomah County Sheriff's Department."

A single door on the opposite side of the counter in the middle of the room stood wide open. Natural light seemed to fill the large space beyond, making it brighter than the office, which flickered under a fluorescent bulb. A dingy watercooler sat on the corner of the counter, and a single armchair with a large rip on the back seemed to fill the rest of the room. Dust layered the once white slats of the blinds, and several dead bugs baked on the windowsill.

She took an involuntary shuffle toward Jeremy, trying to remember if the office had been this dilapidated the last time she was here. It was clear by the look on his face that he wanted to know the same thing, but he remained silent.

"Hello!" he called again, before walking toward the open door.

A face appeared out of nowhere around the door frame, and Jeremy jumped. "Whadya want?"

Jeremy leaned away from the head that didn't appear to have a body. Reaching for his belt, he pulled off his badge. "Multnomah County Sheriff's Deputy, Jeremy Latham."

The other man's eyes grew almost comically large as he shuffled to stand directly in the door frame. Backlit by the sunlight from the windows in the hangar beyond, his name, although sewn onto his shirt, wasn't visible. He poked his tongue out of the corner of his mouth, crossing his arms over his chest.

"Geoff Conner." He pointed his thumb at himself. "You here about that chopper that crashed?" He asked the question of Jeremy but looked past the other man, his eyes raking up and down Heather, giving her chills despite her long-sleeved sweatshirt.

Jeremy took a quick step to the left, blocking Geoff's view and commanding his attention at the same time. "Yes. Did you know the pilot, Jack Dewit?"

Geoff rubbed his chin, his fingers scraping loudly against two- or three-day stubble. "Sure. There're only four of us working here. Course I knew Jack."

"Was he a good pilot?"

"I guess. Been flying more'n twenty years. Never had an accident up until now."

Geoff's gaze wandered again to Heather's blond curls, so Jeremy's voice snapped to grab his attention. "Are you sure it was an accident?"

Bushy eyebrows wrinkled in suspicion, but before Geoff could say anything a cool voice behind Heather answered the question. "Of course it was an accident. Why would you imply it was anything else?"

Jeremy spun around smoothly, as Heather clattered

noisily. Behind her stood a silver-haired man that she'd seen when she'd last been in this office, but she couldn't remember his name. Jeremy quickly introduced himself, flashing his badge.

Before introducing himself, the other man gazed across the room and said, "Geoff, get back to work. Take care of that mechanical problem we're having with the R44. It's got to be ready as soon as we can start tours again." After the younger man bobbed his head and disappeared, the other continued, "I'm Newt Martinson. I own PNW."

The tension in the air was palpable, and it surprised Heather. But Jeremy wasn't thrown at all. "Mr. Martinson, we're investigating the crash of your helicopter and wondered if we could take a quick look around."

"Do you have a warrant?"

"No, we don't. We just wanted to look at where you stored the chopper that went down."

Martinson's eyes narrowed, and his voice came out a near growl. "Not without a warrant."

Heather stepped forward, imploring the other man to show some kindness. "Do you remember me? I was—"

"I know who you are. And I'm very sorry that your sister died, but I have nothing else to say to you without my lawyer present." He rocked back on his heels, and added as an afterthought, "To either of you." He inclined his head toward the front door, inviting them to leave.

They took the not-so-subtle hint; and once back on the road, Jeremy caught her gaze in the mirror. "How did you end up using them for your tour?"

She shook her head and shrugged. "Kit knew someone. We got a good deal, and..." She swallowed, trying to dislodge the lump that suddenly formed at the memory of her conversation with Kit about PNW. On the morning of the crash, they'd laughed about the condition of the office, but it hadn't mattered since they were together, the first real together time their schedules had allowed in months.

Jeremy jumped in, his voice soft. "I think Martinson is hiding something. I don't know about Geoff, but something at that place isn't right."

"I know. But do you think it's the drugs?"

He shrugged, again falling into the silence that had reigned on and off all afternoon. They both seemed to need time to think through the questions that didn't have answers. But for Heather, all of the unanswered queries really only led to the singularly important one. Would Kit's killer pay for what he'd done?

God, please let me do my part to bring him to justice.

The words bounced around in her mind, but didn't even penetrate the roof of the car. Again her prayers fell flat, useless.

Closing her eyes in frustration, she didn't see what made Jeremy slam on the brakes so hard that her head banged into the back of his headrest.

Rubbing the stinging on her forehead, she looked up at her house, which had matched the neighboring townhomes when they'd left that morning. Now the two front windows on either side of the door were only jagged shards of glass. And in deep red paint someone had left a message that couldn't be misinterpreted.

YOUR DEAD.

NINE

"Stay in the car." What Jeremy had intended to be a firm instruction came out a growled demand, but blood roared so loudly in his ears that he couldn't hear if Heather even responded. He checked his service weapon, his grip sure and steady as he slipped from the car. The door clicked closed almost inaudibly, and he was already bounding up the steps. His tennis shoes tapped lightly on the cement as he leaned into the town house's door.

The smell of fresh paint assailed him, and he adjusted his position just before putting his shoulder into the sticky, red mess. Instead he toed the door open, which he hadn't noticed was already ajar until he was right next to it.

He took a small step, and immediately glass crunched under his foot. His gaze quickly found the broken light bulb in the lantern above the black iron mailbox. Taking another tentative step, he landed in a relatively safe place and pushed farther into the darkness.

His elbows tight but not locked, Jeremy held his weapon in front of him as he tiptoed through the kitchen and peeked into the bathroom. Then he went into the bedroom, nearly stumbling over Heather's bed. After checking that the closet was empty, he slipped back into the living room.

Suddenly a floorboard creaked, and he spun toward the front door, where Heather had appeared, leaning on her crutches, but also holding her Glock, an extra that she'd pulled from her gun safe. Against the pale streetlights, he could only make out her silhouette as her hand danced along the wall.

Compared to the inky darkness, the abrupt overhead light burned his eyes. Fighting the spots that danced behind his eyelids, his gut clenched when he heard a solid footstep coming from the area by the bathroom.

Before he could open his eyes, a solid body slammed into him, sending him to the floor. Immediately he reached for the assailant's jeans-clad leg, but with a quick hop the other man evaded capture, only one person between him and freedom.

Praying that Heather would step aside and be spared another injury, Jeremy pushed himself to his feet just in time to see the masked man kick Heather's knee and disappear out the door. She crumpled into a heap, her crutches banging to the tile floor. In a moment, he knelt beside her, gently unfolding her limbs and letting her rest her head on his chest.

"Are you hurt? Do I need to call an ambulance?"

"I think…" Her breathing was fast and shallow, as though she couldn't catch it after running a 10K. "I think I'm okay. Just need a minute."

He nodded, brushing long, blond curls from her face and tucking them behind her ears. He read pain across her features in the tight lines around her eyes and mouth, and her grip on his hand threatened to cut off circulation.

After several minutes of kneeling on the hard floor,

his knees began to ache. Still he didn't move for fear of causing her more pain.

Finally her hand on his loosened and the lines around her lips began to disappear one by one. Then one blue eye opened. She looked around the room, and he could see the question forming in her mind before she spoke a word. "Why didn't you go after him?"

"Well…" Good question. Just one he didn't have an answer for. Truthfully the thought of chasing the intruder hadn't even crossed his mind. "I had to make sure you were okay. I don't have much of a case without you."

That earned him a wavering smile and a trembling pat on his forearm. "Liar."

He grinned. "Okay. I just figured someone who announces his really bad grammar by painting across the front of a house can't be that hard to find."

She chuckled, then wheezed, tucking her arm around her middle. "I think my crutches bruised my ribs on the way to the floor."

"Now that takes talent," he said, barely containing his own laugh. "If you're okay, let's get you up to the couch. Then I'm going to call the police."

She nodded as he helped her sit up. Though his knees cracked as he stood, he bent and scooped her over to the couch. When she was settled, a pillow keeping her knee at an obtuse angle, he asked again, "Do you want me to call for an ambulance? Or I can call the doctor?"

"He didn't really connect with my knee, only the brace. It just surprised me more than anything else."

Now who was lying? But he let it slide, calling the direct line to the police station and asking for Tony. When Jeremy had filled his friend in on the incident, he flipped his cell phone closed and returned to Heather's side. Slipping into the seat by her shoulders, he put an arm around her, holding her shaking form close.

She turned her head into the crook of his arm, but it took several moments before he realized that the dampness there was from her tears. Coaxing her face toward him, he thumbed away a few stray drops.

Holding her gaze, he said, "It's going to be all right."

"How can you be so sure?" She looked away and swallowed thickly. "It wasn't all right for Kit. These people... they're willing to kill for whatever it is they want. And I can't even defend myself." Bitterness entwined itself in her last words as she tapped her injured leg. Frustration and fear seeped from her pores, but it wasn't hers to bear.

"It was my fault tonight. I didn't look behind the bathroom door. He must have been in there." It would have been so easy to lose Heather like he'd lost Reena. And there could be no denying his failure to protect the woman in his care. His throat tightened, but he continued. "I'm so sorry."

She probably didn't know what to say, but her drying eyes met his as she shook her head. "This isn't your fault. Unless you sent that bad-grammar guy here, you're not responsible for any of this."

The chortle that burst out of him shocked them both, bringing small smiles. Heather blinked, thick lashes resting against her pale cheeks for just a moment. When she opened her eyes, she leaned toward him, resting one hand on his biceps.

He knew he shouldn't confuse the situation any more than it already was. Knew that they needed to stay focused on the person trying to kill her. Knew that she deserved better than a man who couldn't protect his own.

And he threw all of that out the window the moment she trapped the corner of her bottom lip between perfect white teeth.

Their lips connected briefly at first, like a feather's touch. When he hesitated, she kissed him again, more insistent the second time, her lashes brushing his cheeks. He plunged his fingers into the softness of her unruly curls, holding her head steady.

She felt like comfort and renewal, reassurance and compassion in his arms. After their trying day, he needed this link. And he forgot every reason not to hold on to her forever.

Until someone knocked on the partially open door and cleared his throat loudly.

Heather looked up from her folded hands in her lap into the deep brown eyes of Jeremy's friend Tony Bianchi. Dressed in street clothes, his service weapon was tucked into a shoulder holster under one arm. He flipped another page in his miniature moleskin notebook, his pen still taking detailed notes after nearly half an hour.

She couldn't imagine that there was anything they hadn't covered in the interview. Now she just wanted sleep. The adrenaline had evaporated and with it her ability to keep her eyes open for more than a few seconds at a time.

Tony tapped his pen on the page of the notebook, his eyes narrowing at the words written there. "You're sure you didn't get a look at the man who was in your house?"

"Like I said, he was about six foot, medium build,

maybe smaller than that. He was wearing a black ski mask. I couldn't see his face. But he was wearing faded blue jeans and a long-sleeved black shirt and black gloves."

Both of their gazes roamed to the front window where black powder still lined shards of glass. They hadn't been able to find even a partial fingerprint because of those gloves. But at least the lack of evidence meant the crime scene didn't have to be preserved, which had allowed Jeremy to nail plywood where the glass had been. He hammered the final nail in place and looked over his shoulder in the direction of the couch.

He seemed to forget that his friend was even in the room, his gaze almost a palpable reminder of his tender kiss. His smile turned knowing, and she felt fire flush her cheeks. Was he thinking about it, too?

His head dipped, and when he looked up again, his grin had vanished.

Suddenly self-conscious about the blush she was sure tinted her cheeks, Heather turned back to Tony, who pushed himself from the couch. "Well, I guess that's everything we need from you, Heather." He stuck his hand out, and she looked at it for a moment, still analyzing what Jeremy was thinking. Finally she realized that Tony was offering to shake her hand, and hers jumped out like something had bit her.

"Thank you, Tony."

His eyes turned soft. "I'm sorry about this, Heather. All of it." Did that include having Jeremy so close and the inner turmoil it was already causing? Probably not, but she still didn't know how to respond.

Jeremy saved her from having to. He walked up, sliding leather work gloves off his hands. The two men shook hands and Jeremy clapped his friend on the shoulder with the other in a completely male stance.

"Thanks for coming out personally. I know you could have just sent someone, but I'm glad that you came."

Tony nodded. "Always good to see you, man." He nodded again at her. "Good to meet you, Heather. I'll call if we hear any news on your case—here and at the hospital."

"Thanks!" she called, as he walked down the steps to the street. Jeremy closed and locked the door behind him and turned to lean against it. His gaze weighed heavily on her, and she put her hands over her face, trying to keep her head from falling off.

Through the cracks in her fingers, she saw Jeremy walk across the room and reach out to touch her shoulder, but he stopped several inches from her arm. His hand remained elevated for several long seconds before it dropped to his side. Clearing his throat, he asked, "How're you doing?"

She spread her fingers a little farther apart and peeked at him through the crack. Then she ventured a quick glance at the loose door handle. "Will that hold tonight?"

"We should be okay. It's flimsy, but we'll get someone out here tomorrow to get it taken care of." His stare didn't stray from her face, and his jaw clenched and unclenched several times. "You didn't answer my question."

How could she possibly answer his question? Of course, she wasn't doing okay. Kit was gone, someone was trying to kill her and she'd bet that same someone had broken into her home. And then there was the matter of that toe-tingling kiss she couldn't stop thinking about from the man sleeping on her couch.

A sigh escaped before she even realized it was coming. "I need sleep."

"You haven't had anything to eat tonight. I could make you something, if you're hungry." He nodded toward the kitchen, but his eyes evaluated her from head to floor, as though looking for evidence that she wasn't telling him the whole truth.

Pushing herself up from the couch, she shook her head.

He rubbed his hands together like he was trying to warm them up. "Listen. About earlier. I'm sorr—"

"Not hungry." She interjected.

Was he seriously about to apologize for that kiss, the one that had nearly made her toes numb and clearly shut off her brain? She couldn't handle hearing those words out loud at that moment, so she used one of her crutches to push past him, mumbling. "Just tired. I'll see you in the morning."

After locking the bedroom door behind her, she threw her crutches on the floor and fell onto her bed, being careful not to jostle her still tender knee.

Not even bothering to change into her pajamas, she rolled under the covers and closed her eyes, willing sleep to come. But all she saw was the perfectly peaceful look on Jeremy's face the moment before he kissed her. Every line on his face had disappeared in the serenity and certainty of the moment, and when he'd held her, it had been bliss. The fear that she'd known since seeing those terrible words scrawled across her home had disappeared in an instant.

And then he tried to say he was sorry for it.

She bit back the angry grumble forming in her throat.

What kind of a jerk kissed like that and then promptly apologized for it?

A cabinet in the kitchen closed, then the refrigerator door. Apparently Jeremy's offer to make food had been more for himself than for her.

She rolled so her back was to the door, but she could still hear him in the kitchen. Pushing hair out of her face, she wished it was as easy to brush Jeremy from her thoughts. Having reminders of him everywhere only agitated her, and she couldn't afford any distractions.

If she didn't see that Kit's killer was rightfully punished, who would?

And if he was after her, all the better. They'd meet someday. Soon.

She just needed to ensure that it happened on her terms.

Thinking about Jeremy and his kiss and the way her pulse skittered whenever she saw him wasn't going to help her have that meeting on her terms, so she pushed thoughts of him aside.

Pushed his thick, brown hair, handsome face and slightly crooked grin into the deepest recesses of her mind.

Too bad it didn't work.

Twenty minutes later she was still trying to push thoughts of him away.

She needed something else to focus on. Opening one eye, she scanned the floor of her room. The white file box from Kit's office sat just within arm's reach. Straining, she wrapped a finger around the handle and tugged it toward her.

The box was heavier than she remembered as she pulled it onto her bed. Scooting to sit up, she reached for the switch on the small lamp on her nightstand. Though muted by a Belgian scarf over the lamp shade, the light still seemed to fill every corner of the room.

Her right knee throbbed, and she pushed a pillow beneath it before setting the lid to the box aside.

"Lord, if there's a clue to solve this case in this box, please let me find it. Help me to pay back the person responsible for stealing Kit away from me." Her stomach clenched, making a knot of her insides, and once again she felt as though she was praying to an empty room. Surely her uneasiness stemmed from the break-in, not from anything wrong with the prayer itself. Solving this case was the right thing to do and her only course of action.

She heaved a loud sigh as she pulled out Kit's nameplate and business card holder. Flipping through, she analyzed the cards for any indication of a message, but the cards were almost entirely for flower shops, dance lessons and dressmakers.

Kit had been planning a wedding. No secret code there.

A few more items fell into the same category, and disappointment clouded Heather's zeal. This was a waste of time.

Until she saw the picture, the one of her and Kit as kids. They were wearing matching yellow tank tops and shorts, playing on the tire swing in their grandparents' backyard. Before going through the box yesterday, Heather hadn't seen the picture in years, barely even remembered that day.

What she did remember was that they had hidden something in that tire and made their grandparents search the yard for it.

This picture hadn't been in the frame the last time Heather visited Kit at her office. She was nearly certain that the frame had held Kit and Clay's engagement picture. So why had she swapped it out? Was there a message for her in that tire?

Doubtful.

But she had to make sure.

Flipping open the tabs on the back of the frame that held the picture in place, she popped out two glossy photos and a carefully folded sheet of yellow legal paper. Just as she'd suspected, the second picture was the same one Clay's mother had insisted on submitting to the newspaper's society section.

But it was the paper that captured her interest. When she had unfolded it, she discovered that it actually contained three pages, each covered in scribbled notes in Kit's handwriting.

Her eyes skimmed the pages as fast as she could read, but there were no details, only paraphrases and numbers that didn't make sense at this time of night.

A loud snore suddenly came from the living room, reminding her that Jeremy was there. She'd been so angry with him earlier that part of her wanted to ignore him, keep this breakthrough to herself. But her aggravation from earlier didn't matter anymore. She needed his help to decipher these notes.

Rolling until her feet hit the floor, she pushed herself past her crutches, determined to make it to the kitchen table without them. She flung open the bedroom door just as Jeremy released another snort.

"Get up!" she called, half walking, half hopping past his reclined form on the couch. He groaned, opening one eye and pulling his blanket farther under his chin.

"What's going on?" He ran long fingers through tousled brown locks and blinked when she flipped on the kitchen light, sitting up to reveal a wrinkled white

T-shirt. Leaning on his arms pulled the fabric around them taut, but she didn't look at that.

Much.

"I found something in the box from Kit's office. It's notes." She waved the papers back and forth, the sound of crinkling paper filling his stunned silence.

"What do they say?" Scrambling from his makeshift bed, he was by her side in an instant.

"I don't know." She huffed. "They don't make much sense. I thought you might want to help me figure them out."

He immediately pulled out a chair and sat next to her, but before diving into the yellow papers, he looked around, slightly confused. "Where are your crutches?"

She shrugged. "I didn't have time for them."

His mouth turned up on just one corner. "How's your knee?"

"Just fine, thank you." She knew she didn't sound very thankful, but that was okay. She didn't feel very thankful, either. His eyes turned mischievous, so she thrust a single page at him. "Just look at this. Let's figure out what she was trying to tell us."

They poured over the pen scratches for nearly fifteen minutes in complete silence, taking turns with each page. Flipping sheets over. Shaking their heads. Flipping them over again.

At best it seemed to be an incoherent concoction of dates and names and sometimes just single letters. No verbs. No action.

Nearly ready to pull her hair out, Heather jumped when Jeremy said, "Where did you find these?"

"Behind a picture in a frame."

His lips pursed and eyes squinted into the distance.

His fingers strummed the table in perfect rhythm. "So she hid these notes? What if she was worried that someone was going to find them?"

Heather nodded slowly, her chin bouncing in her hand, elbow resting on the table. "What if they're written so cryptically just in case that person ever *did* find them? What if we just have to figure it out?"

He nodded, pointing to a date splashed across the top of what they assumed was the first page. "See, where it says P-55. Then at the bottom of the page, N-543. And on the last page, W-78."

Like a cloud lifting, it became clear. "That's the phone number for PNW, isn't it?"

He punched the number into his phone and nodded to confirm when a recorded voice came on the other line. "So if the individual letters added up to a company name, then it would stand to reason that the other letters are initials as well." He put his finger under a capital F halfway down the second page. After the F, Kit had written *involved* and followed it with a question mark with an X through it. "Could this be a Frank, or a Fred?"

"I don't know. But it sure looks like she had confirmed that F was involved."

After another ten minutes, they'd been able to figure out only one other name and phone number combination.

"Well, Mr. Mick Gordon, is it?" Heather said more to herself than Jeremy. Reaching for her phone, she pressed in the numbers.

Jeremy's gaze shot to the clock on the microwave. "You're going to call him now?"

It was well after one in the morning, but Heather just shrugged as she turned the phone onto Speaker and set it on the table between them. "Maybe we'll catch him off guard."

The phone rang three times on the other end before a very groggy voice answered. "Yes?"

"Mick Gordon?"

The silence then was thick and pregnant with unsaid words.

"Who is this?" the man asked.

Heather leaned in toward the phone, speaking slowly and clearly. "My name is Heather Sloan, and I want to know why someone is trying to kill me."

TEN

The sun peeked through Heather's bedroom window the next morning, but she hadn't been able to turn her mind off all night for replaying the brief conversation with Mick Gordon over and over.

"I want to know why someone is trying to kill me," she had said.

He spluttered inelegantly, his voice cracking on the first syllable. "I don't know what you mean."

She looked across the table at Jeremy, suddenly uncertain about her rash decision to call the only contact they'd been able to decipher in Kit's notes. He motioned for her to continue but made no sound to give away his presence.

"Yes, you do. You knew my sister, Kit, didn't you?"

He was silent so long that Heather thought Mick might not respond, but finally, he said, "We met."

Heather rolled her eyes at his evasive maneuver. "I think Kit was looking into a case that she was keeping very quiet. Did you help her out with that? Maybe give her some information?"

"No."

Heather squeezed her fists until her knuckles turned white, glaring from Jeremy to the phone and back.

Finally, Jeremy scribbled something on a blank corner of one of the yellow sheets of paper, and he spun the paper so Heather could read it.

Try a different direction. Ask him about PNW.

"Mr. Gordon—" she took a deep breath through her nose letting it out slowly, hoping her voice came out soothing and not how she really felt "—have you heard of a sightseeing company called PNW?"

"Course I have. They've been in the news lately."

She strangled a pained sigh before it could escape. "Had you heard about them before the recent helicopter crash?"

"Maybe."

Jeremy's head perked up, and he nodded slowly, his hands making slow rowing motions in front of him. Heather nodded, taking her time to ask the right question, terrified of losing the tenuous connection she'd forged with the man on the other end of the phone.

"My sister knew someone at PNW, but she never told me who it was. Did you know the same person there?"

"I don't know. She didn't tell me who she knew there."

"What did she tell you?"

The man swallowed audibly, and Heather rubbed her face with open hands, realizing for the first time that night that she was really tired. Struggling to keep a yawn at bay, she let her eyes dart to Jeremy, who watched her with unblinking eyes. While tempted to let her thoughts wander to what had kept her from falling asleep in the first place, Mick's quiet voice brought her focus right where it should be.

"She said she thought there was more going on at PNW than sightseeing tours. Your sister said she was going to prosecute the people involved and me, too, if I didn't cooperate."

"So you cooperated? What did she have on you that would have sent you to jail?"

"I told her everything I knew about the drugs, but I didn't mean…" His voice got so quiet that she couldn't hear him.

"Mick? Are you still there?"

He was silent a long time before he sighed. "Yes."

"What didn't you mean?"

"I never wanted anything bad to happen to her. I liked your sister. She wasn't mean or nothing. She just had to know what was going on. But it's my fault."

"What's your fault?"

"They killed her because of what I said."

"But what *exactly* did you say?" She tugged at the roots of her hair, the muscles in her back and arms taut with anticipation. "Tell me what you said and about how that got her killed."

"If I tell you, they'll try to kill you, too." She tried to interject that they were already after her, but his words erupted in a deluge. "I can't have another death on my conscience."

"But they're already trying to kill me," Heather said as the illuminated screen on the phone flashed *Call Ended*. She heaved a sigh and threw her forehead onto her folded arms resting on the table.

Devoid of hope and dragged down by useless limbs, she wasn't sure how she could possibly move again, but it was Jeremy who had wordlessly helped her to her feet and guided her to her bedroom door, telling her to get some sleep.

Sleep only came in snippets that night, but as the sun climbed the morning sky, it beckoned her to rise as well. Stumbling out of bed, she tugged her robe on over yesterday's wrinkled clothes. Pushing through the twinges in her knee, she stepped over her crutches and used the door frame to steady herself before hobbling toward the kitchen.

Jeremy stood at the coffeemaker, his back to her, but holding out her polka-dotted mug. Steam curled above the rim, and she smiled as she pulled it to her lips. "Morning," he said, finally looking up from his paper. His red-rimmed eyes weren't quite open all the way, and he hadn't managed to shave a day's worth of dark stubble on his chin, but his damp hair and clean clothes at least announced that he was partially ready to face the day.

"The lab called this morning and confirmed that the powder at the crash site is cocaine."

Her face scrunched up as she tried to kick-start her brain. "Okay. Good."

Two toaster pastries popped up in the toaster, and he wrapped one in a napkin before handing it to her. He shoved half of the other into his mouth at once. "What do you think?" he said around the mouthful. "Shall we go find Mick Gordon today?"

"Yes!" She bobbed wild, blond curls.

"Go get ready. Then we'll head over to the sheriff's office and check county records until we find this guy."

Heather yelped as scalding coffee burned her throat, but she gulped down the entire mug and barely rinsed it out in the sink before hobbling quickly to get ready.

As he drove toward the office, Jeremy realized just how much he liked having Heather sitting next to him. He knew he shouldn't focus on it, but she'd been riding in his backseat to accommodate her leg for what felt like weeks. He hadn't known what he was missing when she sat behind him.

Namely a sweet scent that filled the front of the car.

His head ached from lack of sleep, but how could anyone have expected him to get any rest after the way the phone call with Mick Gordon had ended? Heather probably hadn't gotten much shut-eye, either. After that call, they were both eager to find the man who clearly knew more about the case than they did.

Heather yawned loudly, then shot him a guilty look. "Sorry. I didn't sleep well last night."

He grinned. "Me neither." They were silent for several long seconds, and he had a sudden urge to fill the space with something. Anything. "You were good last night. On the phone with Mick, I mean."

"Thanks."

"How's your knee feeling?"

"Better."

He focused on her out of the corner of his eye as he pulled to a stop behind a truck. She didn't seem unhappy, but she wasn't giving him anything to build a conversation on. What could have her so distracted this morning?

She certainly wasn't thinking about their kiss. Was she?

He hadn't been thinking about it.

Much.

Heather's phone rang softly, playing a popular praise chorus that he was pretty sure he'd heard at church the Sunday before. "Hi, Mom." The tension in the car exploded in an instant. The concern radiating off her was tangible. "What do you mean? What time was Clay supposed to call you?" She sucked in her breath, holding it for several seconds before letting it out. "Of course we will." She glanced at him, her voice going softer. "A friend and I will take care of it, and I'll call as soon as I know anything, okay?"

As soon as she hung up, he asked, "What's going on?"

"There's something wrong with Clay."

Jeremy tried to ignore the burning in his stomach at just hearing the other man's name. Maybe it was the way Heather said it, with an affectionate lilt in her tone, but he didn't like it one bit.

Heather continued. "He was supposed to call my mom this morning. She's been checking in with him, just to make sure he's doing okay. But he didn't call, and when she called him, he didn't answer."

"What do you want to do?" he asked as he pulled into the parking lot of the sheriff's office. He didn't bother turning off the car, because no matter how he reacted to Clay's name, he couldn't deny Heather anything.

She shifted in the seat, still hampered by the unwieldy brace, and looked right into his eyes. Sapphire-blue eyes, glassy with unshed tears, blinked slowly, mournfully. "What if they think Clay knows something, too? What if they're trying to kill him?" She swallowed before plunging in again. "What if they've already—"

He reached out for her hand, and laced his fingers through hers. "Don't do that to yourself. Let's focus on what we know and not let our imaginations take over."

She nodded, her eyes still watery. But she didn't let even one tear escape before she sniffed and pulled herself together. Squeezing her hand, he tilted his head toward the road. "Tell me where I'm going."

Heather clung to his hand, nearly cutting off circulation, as she gave him basic directions to Clay's house. Jeremy tried to squeeze hers back in reassurance, but he wasn't sure she could feel anything at that point.

As they started the twenty-minute journey toward the ritzy neighborhood where Clay lived, Jeremy whispered, *"God, please take care of Clay. Whatever the situation, let us get there in time to help."*

"Thank you," Heather said. Sliding along the seat, she leaned into him and rested her head on his shoulder.

He both loved and hated how perfect she felt there, her hair baby soft against his cheek. As he drove, he nearly forgot why they weren't at the office looking for Mick Gordon. Nearly forgot that pangs of jealousy bombarded him every time Heather said the other man's name.

Nearly forgot that he couldn't let himself enjoy this, couldn't allow himself to become a permanent part of Heather's life when he hadn't been able to save her from a break-in the night before.

It was all too familiar, leaving the woman in his life to fend for herself because he'd failed to protect her.

The muscles in his shoulders tensed, and he felt Heather's muscles tighten beside him in response.

"You worried about what we're going to find?" she asked.

Not really. "Just thinking."

"About what?"

He wasn't about to spout off about the tragic memory, and he didn't want to talk about his involuntary reaction to Clay's name. Turning the wheel into an upper-crust subdivision of identical two-story homes with neutral paint and pale green trim, he sighed. "Nothing much.

Just about how we met only six days ago, but you've become a big part of my life."

"Me, too." She threaded an arm through his and snuggled a little deeper. "Thank you for doing this." She swallowed so loudly that he could hear it. "You're doing so much more than you have to, and I appreciate it."

He opened his mouth to respond, although he didn't have any idea what to say. But as he pulled into the driveway of the address Heather had directed him to, his mind went blank at the all-too-familiar sight of the front door standing open.

Heather's head shot off his shoulder, and she clattered out of the car before he could even turn it off.

"Clay!" she called as she swung up the front walk faster than he'd ever seen her move. Her hair swayed from side to side with each step, and he chased behind her, the lack of response from inside the house making his stomach roll.

"Clay, where are you?" Heather yelled just before reaching the door and smashing it open with the rubber tip of her crutch.

She stopped so suddenly that Jeremy ran into her back and had to grab her waist to keep her from falling forward. As he peered over her shoulder, he saw what he knew she feared most. Clay's limp form lay in the foyer, a trickle of blood rolling down his forehead.

ELEVEN

"**S**tep back!" Jeremy commanded. His hands on her shoulders moved her to the side, as he stepped past her. "Call nine-one-one."

Heather fumbled for her cell phone, punched the wrong buttons twice and finally connected. "Is he alive?" she whispered as the ringer on the other end sounded in her ear.

Oh, God, please let Clay be okay. I know my prayers haven't been worth much lately. They don't seem to be making it over my head, and I'm sure that's my fault. I just... Please, let him be all right.

"Nine-one-one, what is your emergency?"

"My sister's fiancé was attacked."

"Ma'am, where are you?"

Heather scrambled in her brain, staring at the green numbers on the house for a full second before she spit out the address. "Please, he's bleeding."

"Is he breathing?" Her voice was so calm, and Heather hated it. She wanted the other woman to understand her urgency, to see that her life was falling apart.

Jeremy kneeled next to Clay, two fingers on his neck. Then he leaned over, his cheek just inches from Clay's face. When he straightened, the lines on his face had relaxed. "He's breathing, and his pulse is strong."

"Yes," Heather sighed into the phone in response to the woman's question. "But he's unconscious. His head is bleeding."

"I'm sending an ambulance out to this address right now. Please stay on the line until help arrives."

Heather leaned against the door frame, letting her arm drop to her side, but not hanging up the phone. Her eyes locked with Jeremy's as he pulled a blue paisley handkerchief from his pocket and pressed it against Clay's forehead. "He's going to be okay," Jeremy said. "Probably just a concussion and a couple stitches."

At just that moment, Clay's long black lashes fluttered and he squinted up at them, his face pinched in pain. His expression changed from confusion to understanding as his gaze moved from Jeremy to Heather.

"Heather," he breathed.

"I'm here, Clay. I just can't get down next to you right now."

He made a move to nod, but Jeremy's hand on his head kept him firmly in place. "How long have I been out?" Suddenly he wheezed a cough and grabbed his stomach, groaning.

"Stay still," Jeremy said, his free hand on the other man's arm keeping him in place.

A purple bruise on Clay's chin began to take shape, and Heather winced. "What happened to you?"

Clay closed his eyes, leaning back onto the plush carpet. "I was expecting my housekeeper." His chest heaved with the effort it took him to finish his thought. "I thought it was her. Someone crashed in when I opened the door. Hit me on the head. Must have kicked me in the ribs."

His breathing became more labored, and finally Jeremy said, "Calm down. Don't talk." He looked up at Heather for confirmation. "An ambulance is on the way, and we'll go to the hospital with you. So just hang on."

And then sirens came, first a police cruiser and then an ambulance. Heather said goodbye to the operator on the other end of the line and walked with the EMTs as they rolled Clay out on a stretcher.

The young, dark-haired medic eyed Heather's leg brace as she moved to join Clay in the vehicle's bay. "Ma'am, were you injured, too?"

"What? Oh, no. I had surgery on my knee. I'm fine. I just need some help to get up there." Before the older EMT could reach for her, a pair of strong hands hoisted her smoothly onto the single available seat and set her crutches next to her. She turned to give Jeremy a smile, but he was already backing away toward his own car.

"I'll meet you at the hospital, okay?"

"Thank you," she whispered, hoping he could read her lips, as she was sure he wasn't able to hear her at that distance.

The doors slammed shut, and the younger EMT continued giving care to Clay. But Heather couldn't seem to tear her gaze away from Jeremy through the window and kept her eyes on him until they turned a corner and he disappeared. Then she rested her hand on Clay's ankle, as they bumped along toward the hospital.

True to his word Jeremy was there as soon as the bay doors opened. Not even waiting to be asked, he reached for her and helped her land gently on her feet, then secured her crutches in place before stepping back.

In a flash the medical staff swarmed toward them, and they shuffled out of the way, watching as Clay's stretcher was whisked away. One of the E.R. nurses asked them to wait in a small room, so they found two moderately comfortable chairs and settled in.

Jeremy didn't say anything for so long that Heather finally broke the silence. Nudging his knee with her good one, she said, "Do you really think he'll be okay?"

He patted her forearm, the heat from his palm making it all the way to her shoulder and sending goose bumps down her back. Her mind immediately jumped to the kiss the night before, but she tried to block it out.

"He'll be fine. The doctors will take good care of him."

But what if it was related to the crash and the break-in at her house? If so, Clay was still in danger of being attacked again. Terrified that he would confirm her worst fear, she didn't want to ask his opinion, but she had to know. Knowing was better than just worrying, right?

And nearly as important as having her questions answered, why wasn't he reading her mind and giving her the response she longed for?

She looked at the stubble on his cheek, then lifted her gaze to his, willing him to see her worry there. His eyebrows came together, but he didn't say anything.

Finally she leaned closer to him. "Well…"

"Well, what?"

"You know what!" Her voice rose a whispered octave. "Tell me what you're thinking."

He shook his head, running his hand over her hair and cupping the back of her neck. "I told you when we first met, I don't believe in coincidences."

She shrank away, her shoulders hunching to keep out the realization, the news she knew she needed to accept. Squishing her eyes shut, she tried not to see

Clay's bleeding and prone body, but she couldn't wipe that image from her mind.

Jeremy cupped her cheek with his palm, lifting her face toward him, but he didn't say anything until she opened her eyes.

"Heather, I know this difficult, but you and I both know that Clay is now involved in this case."

"Did they—that is, do you think Kit told him something about the drugs?"

Jeremy shook his head. "I don't know."

"I'll ask him."

Jeremy's face turned dark, as though a cloud had passed over it. "I'd rather you not."

"Why shouldn't I?"

"He's a civilian." Jeremy shrugged. "Okay, that reason feels a bit thin even to me, but I'm worried about too many people finding out how much we know. Maybe we don't know anything. Maybe we're on the verge of cracking the whole case open. Either way, if Clay inadvertently spilled our info to someone else, word could get around.

"Plus, what if Kit never said anything to him about it? There's no need to get him worked up when he just needs to focus on recovering. After all, it doesn't really matter if Kit said something to him, which I'm sure he would have told us about by now if she had. Clearly they think he knows something."

Her lips pursed to the side, and she nodded. "All right. But we have to find Mick Gordon."

"Agreed. Have you tried calling him back?"

"Yes." She rolled her eyes, recalling her fruitless efforts that morning. "But let me try again." She pulled out her phone, redialing the number from the night before. It rang and rang but no one picked up and no voice mail system clicked in. She shook her head, turning the phone off.

If only she could call someone at the Bureau and ask them to trace the number. But she wasn't supposed to be working on this or any case. Ignoring Nate's strict instructions meant not only jeopardizing her standing at the Bureau and her friendship with Nate, but also her job.

"We'll find him," Jeremy said. "As soon as we get word on Clay, we'll head over to the sheriff's office and search county records."

"Thank you." She sighed just as a nurse in blue scrubs ambled up to them.

"Are you the family of Clay Kramer?"

Jeremy stood quickly, helping Heather up as well. "We're his friends. Can we see him?"

The middle-aged nurse nodded. "He's in room 3B, down that hallway. He's still a little dazed from the concussion. The doctor wants to keep him overnight to monitor him, but he should be able to go home tomorrow."

Heather leaned into Jeremy's side, relief hitting her so hard it made her weak.

Whoever was trying to take out members of her family hadn't succeeded this time, but they weren't safe as long as he was free. She owed him for everything he'd taken from her, and she was going to pay that debt.

Only the knowledge that the coffee in his foam cup would burn him if it fell on his legs kept Jeremy from crushing it in his fist. He wanted to throw it across the room, but the other deputies at their desks wouldn't appreciate that, either.

He glared at the computer screen again and growled. Mick Gordon didn't exist. There was no sign of the man ever having a driver's license in the state of Oregon, let alone Multnomah County. He'd never rented or purchased property in the area, and no one in the county by that name was paying taxes.

After nearly two hours of searching, he was right where he'd started, with a name and a phone number.

At least he'd sent a sleepy-eyed Heather home with another deputy, who had promised to wait in his car outside her house until Jeremy made it back. As usual Heather had initially refused to cooperate, but when a giant yawn cracked her jaw and made her blue eyes disappear beneath drooping lids during her argument, she'd reluctantly agreed to get some rest if he promised to call her the minute he found out anything.

Now the phone on his desk rang, and he yanked it up. "Latham."

"Hey, man. It's Greg."

"Please tell me you have some good news." Jeremy hated that pleading tone in his voice, but he couldn't help it. He'd asked the other deputy to track the phone number they had for Gordon. "I need a break in this case. What do you have for me?"

"It's a number for a disposable cell phone."

"Like the kind you can pick up at any grocery or convenience store?"

"Just like that."

Jeremy ran his hand over his face, fingernails catching his whiskers. "It's not registered? No way to track it? No GPS on it?"

"Nope. I'm sorry."

"Any chance it could have been paid for with a credit card?"

"I thought you'd ask, so I checked with the convenience store that sold it. They can't track which phone number goes with which purchase."

Now he had a name and no phone number. Mick had probably ditched the phone and even if he'd kept it, he'd sure never answer it as long as he thought Heather might call again.

"Perfect." He managed to hang up the phone without slamming it. Barely. Snatching the nearest piece of paper on his desk, he crumpled it into a ball and chucked it at his trash can as hard as he could. It missed. "Just perfect."

He leaned his elbows on the desk, face in his palms. His stomach twisted painfully. He knew this feeling all too well. Knew what it was like to fail miserably in protecting the person he was supposed to take care of.

Suddenly his cell phone buzzed in his pocket.

"Hey, Tony," he said, picking up. "Do you have some news on the case? Any idea who broke into Heather's place last night?"

"Nothing new. Just calling to check in. How are you both doing?"

Jeremy sagged back in his wheeled desk chair. "Heather didn't get much sleep last night, understandably, so I sent her back to her place to get some rest. She was about ready to fall over."

Jeremy could hear the smile in Tony's voice when he said, "Seems like you've been spending a lot of time with her lately."

"Cut it out, man." Jeremy had known Tony for years, and while they had a strong professional relationship, they were also close enough to rag on each other. Jeremy usually didn't mind being on the receiving end, but something about the current situation set him on edge.

"Hey, I'm just kidding."

"I know. I'm just strung tighter than usual."

Tony seemed to be waiting for Jeremy to continue, but he didn't. Finally Tony said, "You want to talk about it?"

"Not really."

That wasn't true. The memories of Reena and the reality of Heather felt like ulcers brewing in his stomach. They left a wake of headaches and heartbreak. He didn't want to think about them. But as long as he remained silent on the subject, his distress was going to continue.

Maybe Tony had dealt with something similar and could give him some advice, help him deal with the situation until the case was solved and he could remove himself from Heather's life.

Jeremy cleared his throat. "Actually…" Tony waited again, this time not breaking the quiet. "I'm staying on Heather's couch right now, ever since she was released from the hospital. With her injury and someone clearly trying to kill her, I wasn't comfortable without her having someone else in the house overnight."

"Sure. Makes sense. So what's the problem? You don't want to be there anymore?"

"No!" Jeremy clamped his mouth shut, looking around to make sure the other desks in the general vicinity were empty. There was only one other deputy at his desk on the opposite side of the room, but it was enough to make Jeremy stand and walk toward one of the small interrogation rooms where he could have complete privacy.

"I mean, I want to be there," he continued. "I want to protect her, but I don't think I'm the best guy to do that."

"Why not? You're a sheriff's deputy. You're qualified

and competent. Besides, you're already involved in the case. Why would someone else be better?"

Tony's tone was earnest and understanding, and Jeremy had to make a decision. Either he would tell his friend the thing that no one else in Portland knew and possibly get help. Or he'd push it back down and hope time would deal with the pain.

Except it had been five years, and he still hadn't forgiven himself.

Clearing his throat, he leaned on the table. He ruffled his hair with one hand then rolled his neck several times. "Before I moved out here, I made some mistakes."

Jeremy could almost see the man on the other end of the line straighten up, instantly alert. "What kind of mistakes?"

"The kind that I'll regret for the rest of my life."

"Maybe you'd better start from the beginning."

It was do or die. Time to tell the truth or run. "Did you know I was engaged?"

"I didn't know that."

Tugging on his earlobe, Jeremy said, "Reena was fantastic. We met at a Bible study in college, and I was head over heels for her from the start. When I graduated and got a job with the FAA, my life seemed stable, and I was ready for all of it. Marriage. A family. The works. When I proposed, she said yes right away. I think she was as in love as I was.

"And then we went to a Fourth of July picnic at a friend's house. Brad had a little Cessna Skyhawk. It only sat four, so he was going to take Reena and another couple up for a short ride."

Jeremy's stomach plummeted to his knees, and he cringed just thinking about what he was about to say aloud. In fact, he'd never admitted it before to another soul. But Tony was a safe sounding board, and now that he was rolling, he wasn't sure he could stop.

"Brad was helping Reena into the plane when he just happened to mention that he'd replaced a steering gauge earlier that week. Brad was a good pilot and an even better mechanic, but I should have said something. I should have stopped him and asked him which parts he'd used, because I knew. I knew there had been a recall."

Tony sighed loudly, then spoke as if his hand covered his mouth. "That's heavy."

"I couldn't do anything after that. I didn't ask. I didn't stop Brad. I just let them take off, and I had to watch that plane crash. By the time the paramedics got to them, they were all gone."

He let out a breath between tight lips.

He'd survived telling the whole story, and the knot in his stomach loosened a fraction. But telling the truth didn't negate the fact that he hadn't saved Reena, and he couldn't protect Heather.

"Listen, man—" Tony's simple words were laced with emotion "—I'm really sorry for your loss."

"Thanks."

"How long ago was that?"

"More than five years ago. It was right before I moved to Portland. I needed a fresh start."

"Oh, I completely get that," Tony said, then paused for a long second. "What I don't understand is how it's related to the case you're working."

Jeremy pushed his chair back so hard that he almost tipped it over and began pacing the tiny, windowless room. "Don't you get it? I didn't protect Reena. I had the opportunity, and I didn't do what I should have. And I haven't been able to protect Heather, either." He stabbed his unruly hair with outstretched fingers.

"First there was the homeless guy in the hospital. Then last night at her house. I didn't check the bathroom. He was hiding in the bathroom, and I missed him! What if he'd really hurt Heather?"

"That could happen to anyone. Besides, you're ultimately not the one in control. Don't beat yourself up over *what ifs* and *might have beens*."

Jeremy leaned into the wall beneath a security camera, resting his forehead against the cool cement blocks. "I wish it was that easy. But I've let down the two most important women in my life."

What? When had Heather become one of the most important women in his life? Sure, he cared about her. But she liked weak coffee, was really grumpy in the morning and was far too independent for her own good. And yet she was smart and kind and beautiful. She made his pulse skitter every time she walked into a room. And he had to admit, she was pretty adorable when she was grumbling about his coffee. Might as well admit it—he was falling for her.

But what did it matter, anyway, if he couldn't protect her?

TWELVE

Jeremy dialed Heather's cell phone with his hands-free setup as he pulled out from the office.

"Hello." Her voice was sweet and just what he wanted to hear after such a completely wasted day of searching for their only lead.

"It's Jeremy."

"Did you find anything?"

He shook his head, then remembered that she couldn't see him. "Only bad news. Gordon's phone was a disposable cell. Unregistered and impossible to trace. No way to even match a credit card receipt."

"Oh." He could almost see her face fall and her shoulders slump.

"What have you been doing? Did you get some rest today?"

She huffed. "I'm fine. I've just been looking at Kit's notes again."

"Find anything new?"

"Nothing. They're just as cryptic as they were last night." She yawned but tried to muffle the sound by covering the phone.

"Did you get any sleep today? I'm sure you're wiped out."

"I'm perfectly capable of taking care of myself and my sleeping needs. You don't have to check up on me all the time. And you can call off your watchdog, who won't move his cruiser from in front of my house."

Jeremy smiled to himself. It was good to have seniority sometimes, if only to be able to have the newbie act as a bodyguard when Jeremy couldn't. "Not until I get back to your place. Sorry."

Her long-suffering sigh could have won an Emmy. "All right. When are you getting back?"

He glanced at his watch. "I think I'm going to run a quick errand, and I'll be there in about an hour. Tops."

"Do you want me to wait dinner for you?"

"Depends. What are you making?"

"Mac and cheese."

He laughed. "No, thanks."

They hung up, and he pulled a U-turn at the next light, taking him in the opposite direction of Heather's house.

Not really able to pinpoint the reason behind turning around, he let the car carry him to the place where they had started the day. The roads free of rush-hour traffic, he arrived at Clay's neighborhood in a matter of minutes, uncertain of what he was looking for.

All he knew was something gnawed on his stomach. He'd missed something. He should have taken note of something.

But what?

As he pulled up to the curb in front of Clay's house, his headlights illuminated two parked Portland PD cruisers. They were both completely dark, so his gaze jumped to the front door, where two uniformed officers stood staring in his direction.

Hopping out of the car, Jeremy lifted his hand in a casual wave. "Hello, officers," he called.

"Evening. Something we can do for you?"

As he approached, Jeremy said, "I'm Jeremy Latham, with the sheriff's office." He held out his badge, and they both squinted at it.

Finally the stocky man with skin the color of mocha met Jeremy's gaze. "I'm Phillips." His head bobbed once to his right. "This is Rizzy."

"Nice to meet you guys." Jeremy shook hands with both of them, then slid his badge back onto his belt. "You know Tony Bianchi?"

Even though the only light in the area came from the bulb above the door, he could clearly see their postures relax. Phillips offered a genuine smile, and half of Rizzy's mouth pulled upward, the other half seemingly paralyzed.

"Sure, we know Tony. He a friend of yours?"

Jeremy nodded. "He's been helping me out a bit on a case that I've been working. You heard about that helicopter crash outside of town last week?"

Jeremy quickly filled them in with a generic version of the case, leaving out everything that really mattered. No mention of the drugs, Mick Gordon or the break-in at Heather's house.

"So what brings you out here tonight?" Rizzy finally asked.

"The sole survivor of the crash, Heather Sloan, knows the guy who was attacked here this morning. He was the fiancé of her sister, the woman who died in the wreck. I told her I'd ask around a little bit to see if there was anything I could find out for her. See if there was any official news I could pass along."

"We were just coming back to make sure the crime

scene guys cleaned up before Mr. Kramer is released from the hospital," Phillips said. "We don't have anything *official* that we can share, but if you want to look around, you're welcome to."

"Really?" Jackpot! "That'd be great."

Jeremy followed the uniforms into the house, the entryway exactly as it had been that morning. Nearly pristine.

He spun around on the spot, his hands on his hips, brain trying to figure out how everything seemed to be in place. Not even the polished brass trash can had been knocked over. "You guys have any idea why Mr. Kramer was attacked?"

"We thought maybe it was a robbery, but we haven't been able to confirm with him if anything was taken."

Jeremy stepped from the foyer into an opulent living room, complete with plush leather armchairs, a wall-mounted flat-screen television and a total entertainment system including a Blu-ray player, digital music port and even two classic turntables.

He whistled low and deep, and Rizzy walked up beside him.

"I know. And you should see the theater room. Twelve leather recliners and a screen that's got to be nearly a hundred and fifty inches."

"Wow. And it wasn't touched?"

Rizzy shrugged. "Not as far as we can tell."

"What about any other expensive items?"

Phillips strolled up to Jeremy's other side and said, "I found an authentic Rolex and several other high-end watches in his bedroom. They didn't even look like they'd been handled."

"You think that's strange?" Jeremy asked, cupping his chin to rub his cheeks with his thumb and forefinger.

Rizzy shrugged. "Who knows? It's not like this is the first time there's been a robbery in this neighborhood."

"But is this the first time nothing was stolen?"

After a few more minutes, Jeremy thanked the two men and walked back toward his car, hands shoved in his pockets, shoulders hunched against a stiff breeze.

Behind the wheel again, he rested his hands at the twelve o'clock position, staring at nothing in particular.

If the attack *had* been an attempted robbery then quite clearly Clay had been the victim of an incompetent robber. Any thief worth his salt couldn't have passed up the state-of-the-art electronics in that house—or the expensive watches, if he'd wanted something more portable. Which only increased the probability that his attack was somehow related to Heather and Kit. But if it was the same guy after them both, why had he trashed Heather's humble town house and not touched anything at Clay's?

Jeremy couldn't answer that question.

But maybe Clay could help him start to piece together how that morning's events fit with the crash and Heather's break-in. Maybe he'd remembered something about his attacker or something that had been said. At this point, anything was better than walking blind.

Starting his car, he pulled out, headed toward the hospital that he'd visited earlier that day. Retracing his steps might just lead to the breakthrough he needed to protect Heather.

Glancing at his watch, he realized he'd spent over an hour at Clay's house, piling up more questions than answers. He was going to be later getting back to Heather than he expected, so he quickly dialed her number.

"Should I be worried about you?" she greeted him.

He laughed. "Nope. Why? Are you?"

Carefully dodging his question, she said, "Where are you?" Beneath her words, he could hear concern and something else. Maybe a hint of panic? From the girl who seemed to always have it together? Not likely.

"I just talked with a couple of guys from the Portland P.D. They were quite talkative, and I'm going to follow up another lead. I'll be back to your place in a little while."

"What kind of lead? Gordon?"

He hated crushing the hope that had replaced anxiety in her tone. "No. Just some things about the break-in at Clay's place this morning." He steered the car onto the freeway, checking over his shoulder for speeding headlights. Then he continued before she could even ask the question he knew was about to spill out. "The officers just aren't sure if anything was actually taken, plus it doesn't look like the place is tossed, so I'm headed to the hospital to see if Clay can remember anything else about the attack."

She hummed for a moment, a habit when she was putting things in order in her mind before speaking. "I just spoke to Clay about an hour ago. In fact, he called right after you did. He said he still can't remember anything useful." When she paused, he heard her fingernails tapping in rhythm on what he assumed was the kitchen table. "But are you thinking that if robbery wasn't the motive, then it has to be the same person who targeted Kit?"

Chills ran across his neck. It made him squirm when she was on exactly the same wavelength, which seemed to be more and more often the longer they worked this case.

"That's exactly what I was thinking."

She sighed. "How can we protect him? I don't have any more room at my place, and it isn't any safer than his."

"We're not moving in with him. I can tell you that much." No way was he crashing on the couch of a guy who made Heather's eyes look so sad and made Jeremy want to punch something.

He pulled into the parking lot at the hospital and turned off the car. "Well, I'm here. I'm going to run up and chat with Clay for just a second."

"All right. Be careful."

"You, too."

"Ha! That's not hard to do with a guard dog parked out front." The miniblinds clinked back into place on the other end of the phone.

"Gonzales still there?" He couldn't keep the humor out of his voice at her annoyance.

"You know he is."

"Okay. Then I'll see you in about an hour."

As he pulled the phone away from his ear, he thought he heard her say, "I've heard that before." He just laughed it off as he jogged through a light drizzle toward the reception desk on the first floor.

"Hi, I'm looking for Clay Kramer."

"I'm sorry," said the middle-aged man behind the front desk. He swiped at the salt-and-pepper hair on his forehead before continuing. "Visiting hours ended fifteen minutes ago."

Jeremy reached into his pocket and pulled out his ID. "I'm Deputy Latham with the sheriff's department. Mr. Kramer was the victim of a crime, and I need to ask him a few questions."

The other man looked carefully at the ID, then up

into Jeremy's face, as though checking to make sure he hadn't stolen the badge. "Hmm. Okay." With the speed of a sloth, the other man pecked the letters on his keyboard. He hemmed and hawed for several excruciating seconds before finally saying, "He's in room 109."

"And where would that be?"

Looking entirely put out, the man pointed to his left. "Past the elevators and through the double doors."

"Thank you." Jeremy even offered the man a genuine smile before striding in the indicated direction. In less time than it had taken the man at the reception desk to look up the room number, Jeremy arrived at the closed door of 109.

Just as he was about to turn the handle, his phone rang. Pulling it from the back pocket of his khakis and sliding into a secluded corner of the hall, he said, "Hello?"

"Latham, it's Gonzales."

"What's going on? Did something happen to Heather?"

"Nothing like that. It's been quiet all night, but I just got a call from dispatch. Conrad needs backup at an attempted robbery. Shots were fired, and I've got to go."

Jeremy let out his breath in a whoosh. At least Heather was all right. And she'd be okay until he could get back to her. "No problem, man. Thank you for being there today."

"Sure." Gonzales hung up, and Jeremy hurried back to Clay's room. After turning the oblong handle silently, he poked his head into the room.

The only bed in the room was empty, the top sheet and blanket hanging off the far edge. He stepped into the room and looked behind a curtain. The door to the bathroom stood wide open, and Clay wasn't anywhere to be seen.

He hustled toward the nurse's station and quickly introduced himself to the young nurse who didn't look like she'd been out of college for more than a year. He asked, "Do you know where the patient in room 109 is?"

She glanced at a clipboard on the desk. "He should be in his room. I just checked on him less than an hour ago."

"He hasn't been released then?"

She shook her head, her face a mask of confusion. "No, of course not. He's being monitored. Why?"

"He's gone," Jeremy said.

Her eyes grew almost comically large. The nurse's white tennis shoes carried her to 109 in an instant, and she flung open the door, searching just as he had. Then her gaze settled on the stand that held a leaking IV bag, tubes with needles still attached dangling uselessly. She immediately turned and ran back to the desk, picking up the phone. Her voice came over the loud speaker announcing a code, but Jeremy couldn't make out the words over the rushing in his ears.

If Clay was gone and he hadn't checked himself out, then maybe he hadn't had a choice about leaving. And if the perpetrator had made his move against Clay, he might just think it was time to take out the other potential witness.

Ignoring the sudden hubbub surrounding the empty room, he bolted for the door.

By the time he reached the parking lot the sky had opened up with fat drops that made visibility dwindle and the ground slippery. He nearly slipped on the asphalt about ten yards from his car but caught himself on the bumper of a red coupe just in time.

Rain still streamed down his cheeks and chin as he squealed out of the lot, windshield wipers squeaking an incessant rhythm as his headlights bounced along the inky pavement. He pressed the accelerator all the way to floor, barely making a sharp turn to get onto the freeway toward Heather.

All of his actions seemed to be on autopilot, and he couldn't bring his mind to actually ask the "what if" that loomed before him. Instead he repeated a single prayer over and over, his tongue moving as fast as it could.

"God, please let me get there in time. Let me get there in time."

He needed to protect Heather. He had to save her.

The pounding in his chest felt like it would cause permanent bruising, but he didn't care. He just had to get there, had to see that she was okay. A phone call wouldn't be enough to calm his racing pulse, but it would have to do for now.

He didn't want to scare her, but he needed to warn her. It might not calm him down, but at least Heather would be prepared if anything happened.

He nearly swerved off the road, suddenly thankful that the other lanes were empty, as he grabbed for his phone in the center console. "Pick up. Pick up. Pick up," he commanded as the phone on the other end rang and rang. Then voice mail clicked on.

Throwing the phone onto the passenger seat, he accelerated through a yellow light and into Heather's neighborhood. Two sharp rights and a left, and he slammed on his breaks in the empty spot in front of the town house, which had been fitted with new windows.

Slamming his car door, he ran for the house. The rain

still obstructing his view, he thought his eyes were tricking him when he saw a shadow cross between Heather's home and the one next door. He glanced at the sky, hoping it might have been a cloud moving in front of the moon, but the moon was completely hidden.

And then he saw what looked like an arm, pumping as though the figure was running. Jeremy slipped on the wet grass, putting his hand down in the mud before regaining his balance and chasing the lone figure that he could finally see was decked out all in black.

Just past the row of shrubs growing along the side of the brick house, Jeremy gave up catching up to the wiry man, tried not to think about what weapons he might have and launched himself with arms outstretched.

THIRTEEN

Heather couldn't tell if the scream she heard was made by a cat or a man, but she grabbed her gun anyway. An entire afternoon and evening alone was a long time for her mind to conjure all sorts of terrible scenarios, and she wasn't about to take any chances.

As soon as she opened the front door, rain splattered inside. The moonless night seemed especially dark without the aid of the front porch light that she hadn't fixed yet. Grabbing the small flashlight on her key ring, she stepped into the rain.

She clung to the railing as she maneuvered down the slippery steps without her crutches, and when she reached the bottom, she suddenly wished she'd brought them with her.

But there was no time for wishing, as she awkwardly limped over the slick lawn toward the side yard, where she thought the scream had come from.

Flashing her little light across the lawn, the beam landed on two men wiggling on the ground. One wore all black. The other, in sopping wet jeans and a dark polo, turned his head toward her.

Squinting into the unending spatter, Heather flicked her light onto the face of the man in jeans. Jeremy!

"What's going on?" she yelled, but they ignored her. The man in black kicked Jeremy's side and scrambled to get away. But Jeremy grabbed his ankle, sending the other man crumbling to the ground and crying out in agony.

She didn't know if the noise in her ears was from the rain or her blood pumping so hard, but she ran anyway. Moving as fast as she could toward the brawl, she flashed her light on the man in black's face. He twisted, dipping his head away from the beam, which gave Jeremy just enough of an opening to push him into the ground with a knee to the back. Meanwhile, she aimed her gun at the assailant.

"Don't move," she commanded. He wiggled, trying to get free and she stepped closer, nudging his shoulder with her bare foot. "I think it's only fair to tell you that I'm not afraid to shoot you. I've had about the worst week ever. Being forced to shoot you couldn't really make it any worse, so do yourself a favor and just lie still. Got it?"

The man grunted, and Jeremy chuckled softly. "You messed with the wrong woman, man." He cinched his handcuffs around the other man's wrists and stood slowly, stretching his back and neck. His breath came in shallow huffs, and he quickly leaned back over, resting his hands on his knees. He wheezed, and pounded on his chest several times.

"Are you okay?" she asked, reaching a suddenly shaking hand toward his shoulder.

"Fine." He wheezed again, and nodded toward the front. "Let's get out of the rain."

Jeremy bent and helped the man in black to his feet. Walking behind him, Jeremy kept one hand on the cuffs at all times. He pulled up slightly, and the shorter man flinched away from the pain in his shoulders.

"You go ahead," Heather said, her words sending rain flying from her lips. "I'm right behind you."

Jeremy took a stuttering breath. "We'll wait." He held out his free arm for her, and she reached for it, grateful to have something stable to use, as her knee felt like it would fall apart at any second.

"Are you sure you're all right?" she asked after he let out another wheeze.

"Just knocked the wind out of me when I tackled him."

Questions rushed through her mind, but she bit her tongue until they were back inside.

As Jeremy closed the door behind their little parade, she realized that he looked more pale than usual, but he no longer gasped for air. He was covered in mud from the chocolate hem of his jeans to the caked slop in his hair. His left arm was particularly dirty, and he shot her a glance of apology at the brown puddles trailing behind him toward the kitchen.

She picked up one crutch from the end of the couch and used it to make her way toward the linen closet next to the bathroom. "I'll get us some towels."

Jeremy and Heather took turns mopping their soggy hair and clothes, one always keeping an eye and weapon on the man who sat with his arms behind his back, head hanging low. He had dark brown hair at the moment, but Heather wasn't entirely sure what real color hid under layers of muck. His face didn't look any better, so she had a bit of compassion for the guy, wiping his cheeks and nose with her towel.

He wouldn't meet her gaze and kept turning away from her, so it was Jeremy who first said, "Geoff?"

She turned a surprised expression on Jeremy. "Do you know this guy?"

He nodded slowly. "Isn't this Geoff from PNW?"

She looked closely at the wrinkles around his eyes. "The mechanic." She grabbed his chin and turned his face into the light. "I think you're right, Jeremy. But what was he doing outside my house?"

Jeremy's shoulders rose and he shook his head. "I think that's a question for our friend here. Geoff?" He glared at the man who he had just tackled. "The lady asked you a question."

Geoff's lips pursed, and he looked like he was going to spit. Heather jumped back, nearly stumbling as pain rocketed through her leg. As he'd taken to doing so often lately, Jeremy was there to save her, his arms strong as he cradled her gently to his side.

She managed a quick peek into his eyes but couldn't read anything there. Her focus seemed entirely occupied with the touch of his hand on her upper arm, where goose bumps had erupted.

Tearing her gaze away from the streak of mud still smudged across his cheek that made him look like a kid who had just been outside playing, she tried to bring her mind back to Geoff. But it was harder than she anticipated.

Jeremy kissed you then apologized for it. He's not interested in anything here except solving the case. And you aren't, either. You have to focus. For Kit's sake.

But her little pep talk didn't do much to help her focus. It wasn't until Jeremy started talking that she was finally able to get her brain back under control and pay attention to more than the butterflies in her stomach.

"What are you doing here, Geoff? And why did you run away from me?"

"I've got nothing to say to either of you," he growled. His throat sounded sore and his face turned sullen. "Either arrest me or let me go."

Heather eased herself away from Jeremy's embrace and pulled up a chair. Sitting down in front of Geoff, she leaned forward. "Will you tell me something?" He shook his head, his mouth a twisted scowl. She ignored him. "How did you know where I live?"

"I didn't. I wasn't looking for you."

Jeremy snickered. "You're a bad liar." He leaned over the top of Heather's head, resting his hands on her shoulders. He smelled like earth and rain, and she closed her eyes to enjoy the scent for just a moment. "Now tell the lady what she wants to hear."

"Fine." Geoff spat when he spoke, and she recoiled farther toward Jeremy. "I thought I'd ask her to tea at the Ritz."

"Gosh, I'm flattered," Heather mimicked his sarcasm. "But first you have to tell me who you work for. Will he be joining us?"

The thin man just shook his head and swore under his breath. "I'm not sayin' nothin'."

"About what?"

"About nothin'."

Their questions went around and around for several more minutes until Heather leaned back to look up at Jeremy's chin. He glanced down, meeting her gaze, and she nodded toward the living room.

When they were alone in the corner of the other room, Jeremy whispered, "What do you want to do? I don't think he's going to give up anything."

"Me neither." She shook her head and looked at her bare feet. "You think a night in the county jail will loosen his tongue?"

A grin broke his solemn features, his white teeth welcome company. "I like how you think, Special Agent Sloan. I think assaulting a sheriff's deputy is worth at least one night behind bars."

A fresh swarm of butterflies filled her middle. He hadn't called her Special Agent Sloan since they first met, and she liked his validation. She liked his smile, too. And his strength. And his kiss. And…

Well, there was no use thinking about any of that.

"I'll be back as soon as I can," Jeremy said as he led Geoff to the front door. "Lock up and try to get some rest. Tomorrow we'll try again."

He wouldn't stop looking for her sister's killer and protecting her, would he?

She liked that about him, too.

Heather woke to a rush of water barreling through her gutters and down the waterspout, a smile still on her face from the night before.

She had been in bed, trying to fall asleep for nearly two hours when she heard the lock on the front door click and the hinge squeak. Footsteps that she immediately recognized at Jeremy's moved through the living room. His keys rattled on the end table, and two quiet thumps had to be his shoes coming off.

Then the door to her bedroom opened, and Jeremy poked his face into the crack. Silhouetted by the living room table lamp, he leaned into the door frame.

"I'm home. You can go to sleep now." His voice carried a smile and his words warmed her chest.

"How did you know I wasn't asleep yet?"

He chuckled low in his throat. "I don't know. I just did." As he pulled the door closed, he whispered, "Good night."

She had yawned and fallen instantly asleep.

Even with the lovely memory still fresh in her mind, she dreaded getting out of bed. Pulling her quilt up to her chin, she tried to burrow deeper into the cocoon of warmth. But they still had so much to do.

After all, they weren't really any closer to figuring out who had killed Kit and come after her and attacked Clay. They didn't have a single, solid lead. No witnesses or even third parties involved on the fringe.

She had pretty much ruined their chances of getting Mick Gordon to talk, even if they could find him. Then there was some mystery man, whose name started with an F. He was definitely involved, according to Kit. But what if Kit had been wrong?

Heather shook her head. It didn't even matter if they couldn't find him. Kit hadn't left a phone number or any way of identifying him other than the letter F.

She rubbed the heels of her hands against her closed eyes and wiped away a few flecks of crust from the corners. Letting out a sigh, she rolled out of bed, grabbing her robe and tiptoeing into the hallway.

From his bed on the couch, Jeremy gave a loud snort and flipped over, making the springs creak. Was his hair wild after a night on the couch? Did his feet stick off one end?

Tempted to answer those and other questions, she tiptoed toward the living room, then realized that she'd just woken up, too. Her hair was completely disheveled, and her breath probably wasn't minty fresh. She ran her tongue over her teeth to confirm.

But why did it suddenly matter? They'd seen each other first thing in the morning. Why was she worried about her appearance this morning?

Oh, she knew the answer, but she didn't want to think

about it. She refused to dwell on that kiss. That sweet, electric kiss. She wasn't thinking about it at all.

Yeah, right.

Spinning toward the bathroom, she hurried to get ready for the day. Only God knew how much time they had before whoever had hired Geoff got close enough to do what they'd intended the whole time.

After a quick shower, she tried to tame her curls, but after several unsuccessful attempts to straighten them decided on a simple braid that at least kept her hair out of her face. She put on a dab of mascara and some pink lip gloss, just in case they had to interview anyone, of course.

As she padded toward the kitchen in her slippers, her knee ached, but the pain wasn't the same sting as it had been just the day before. The crutches still sat in her bedroom, where she wanted them to stay forever.

"Good morning."

She jumped so hard that she spilled the water she'd been pouring into the coffeemaker. "Morning," she mumbled as she wiped the counter with a towel.

"You sleep okay?"

She glanced over her shoulder to see Jeremy stretched out, hands stacked behind his head and feet propped on the opposite armrest. His blanket reached to his mid-chest, revealing a soft-looking gray T-shirt stretched over his shoulders and arms.

"Just fine. You?"

He yawned and ran his hand over his whiskers that were at least two days old. "Okay." He stretched his neck. "Let me just get a shower and a cup of coffee and then let's figure out our next move."

Heather was still standing by the coffeepot waiting for it to finish brewing when Jeremy emerged from showering and shaving, looking and smelling fresh and ready to go. He ran his fingers through damp hair as he grabbed his usual mug and held it out.

She poured him a full cup and one for herself as well, and they settled in at the table. After nearly a minute of complete silence except the occasional sip of coffee, Jeremy finally said, "I don't know what to do. I think we need more help." Heather nodded slowly as he glared into his cup. "Geoff lawyered up, and he's not going to say anything. At least not in time for us to crack this case before…"

He didn't have to finish. They both knew someone was still out there. This was bigger than one man. Certainly bigger than Geoff.

"Is there someone at the Bureau who could help us?" He didn't look at her until he finished the sentence, and then just shot a sideways glance.

Heather shook her head, her forehead wrinkling. "No. I can't go to them."

He nodded, the corners of his mouth turned down and shoulders sagging.

"I mean, I would. But my boss, Nate, ordered me to take it easy and let you take care of this case."

Jeremy snorted. "You haven't been doing such a good job at that, have you?"

"It's not all that simple, and you know it. I have to be part of this investigation. And if Nate finds out I disobeyed him, it could mean my job."

"What about someone else at the office? Could someone at least run some names through the FBI database as a favor to you?"

She put her elbows on the table and her face in her hands, smoothing and stretching the skin over her cheeks as she pulled her hands apart. "Are we really out of options? There must be something we've overlooked. Something new about Clay's assault yesterday. What did he say last night?"

Jeremy's eyes got wide, and he rubbed the back of his neck. "I can't believe I forgot to tell you."

"What?"

"Clay was gone from the hospital last night."

"What do you mean?" Her head spun, but she refused to believe the worst, even if it pervaded Jeremy's tone. "He was discharged?"

"He was gone, gone. The nurse didn't know where he was, and his IV had been pulled out, but not turned off."

Her hand jumped to cover her mouth, and she coughed on a sob. "Where is he?"

Jeremy just shook his head, his eyes never leaving hers. "I don't know. I'm sorry. I got worried about you. If someone took him, then maybe they were after you last night, too. So I flew back here, and then I saw Geoff and then… Well, you know the rest." A sigh escaped his tight lips as he leaned back in his chair. "I am so sorry that I forgot to tell you."

Fear. Anger. Terror. Heather couldn't put her finger on the emotion that surged through her veins, but it demanded action, and she stood up so fast that she sent her chair flying backward to the ground. The clatter seemed deafening in the otherwise silent room.

In an instant Jeremy was by her side, his hand on her shoulder.

She shook it off, taking a shaky step away from him. "Don't. Don't touch me right now."

He nodded and stepped back. "We'll find Clay. We'll get him back." He reached for her again, then his arms dropped like overcooked noodles. "We just have to get a plan."

"No. We have to go get him. Now."

Jeremy's forehead wrinkled. "But we don't know where he is. We don't know who has him."

"I don't care. We have to find him." She hated how her voice rose, but it was so far from her control in that moment.

"I get that." His words turned stern. "But we have to figure out where he is. Let's make a few calls. Try to get back in touch with Gordon. Check with the police to see if they have any leads."

She shook her hands in front of her, her head starting to spin. "I can't just sit here. I have to do something. I have to go look for him."

"You *can* do something. You can call someone at the Bureau and see if they have something on Gordon." He looked right into her eyes, but his were too calm, too stable. He didn't feel the same urgency she did.

Grabbing his arm, she shook it, trying to get him to understand. "I have to go find Clay."

"We'll just waste time if we just go driving around. We have to know where we're going."

"Don't you get it?" Her voice moved up another octave, and trembled on the last word. "I know you don't understand, but I owe this to Kit. I have to find him. I have to save him."

Jeremy turned his head and rubbed the hair on the back of his head. "You're not the only one trying to atone for mistakes, Heather."

"What's that supposed to mean?" she demanded.

His face turned hard, his features like chiseled stone and eyes like granite. "Nothing."

He turned away, but Heather grabbed his elbow and

spun him back around. "What do you mean, I'm not the only one atoning for mistakes?"

"Just what I said." He pushed his fingers through his hair and looked away from her. "Listen, I don't want to talk about this right now."

The boiling blood in her veins was beyond her control, and she didn't know how to respond. Anger over the situation with Clay and confusion at Jeremy's cryptic words, bubbled together in her chest, and she didn't know how to deal with it.

Once upon a time she would have prayed for peace and direction, but lately her prayers had been as effective as a toy boat in a monsoon.

Putting one hand on her hip and pressing the other to her forehead, she turned around. "I can't believe this! You lied about Clay, and then you admit to keeping secrets related to the case."

"No." In a voice like steel, he said, "I never lied to you about Clay. Everything that happened last night just pushed it out of my mind. I was so focused on your safety that I didn't remember about Clay. I'm sorry about that." He shoved his hands into his pockets, turning away from her. "And I'm not keeping any secrets about this case. I promise."

She crossed her arms over her chest. "Then what are you trying to make up for?"

He groaned and took several steps in the opposite direction from her. Leaning his head back and glaring at the ceiling, he said, "I was engaged once, but she died in a plane crash that I could have prevented. And…I don't know. When I got this case, I guess, I thought if I could help you find the person responsible for Kit's death, I'd start to make up for not doing what I should have for Reena."

Heather's stomach churned with emotions she couldn't name and didn't know where to place. "I'm sorry, Jeremy," she said as she turned, uncrossing her arms then crossing them again when she didn't know what to do with them. "But right now the best thing we can do in Kit's memory is find Clay."

"I agree. But we don't know where to go to find him."

"Fine." She hated the way her voice shook. "You figure out where he is. I'm going to go start looking."

Jeremy's eyebrows pinched together, his features strained with aggravation. "You can barely walk. You can't possibly drive yourself."

"Sure I can." To make her point, she grabbed her car keys from the kitchen counter and strode across the living room, surprising even herself with her mobility. Flinging the front door open, she looked back over her shoulder. "I'll be back when I've found Clay."

She staggered down the steps, clinging to the railing and was halfway to the curb when Jeremy caught up with her. His hand on her elbow effectively stopped any forward motion.

"You're not going anywhere alone," he growled.

"Says who?" she seethed through clenched teeth.

Pointing her hand toward her Saturn SUV parked twenty feet away, she clicked the remote ignition button.

Suddenly the entire world exploded as the Saturn ignited in a blinding, deafening blast.

FOURTEEN

For the second time in as many days, Jeremy lay sprawled on the ground, fruitlessly trying to fill his lungs with air. His forearms felt like they were on fire, and smoke burned his nose.

Heather's car had exploded.

Confirming that all of his limbs were still attached to his body, he rolled onto his side. When he tried to push himself off the grass, he discovered his arm couldn't hold any weight. And he couldn't see Heather anywhere.

"Heather?" The only response came from Heather's neighbors as they stepped onto their front porches to see what had caused such a commotion. Their voices rose to a frantic din as they spotted the vehicle consumed in flames, but Jeremy couldn't make out Heather's voice among them. "Heather!" he croaked, his throat already sore from the blast of smoke.

When she still didn't respond, the beating of his heart turned painful. Rolling again to his other side, he tried for a second time to push himself up, but barely made it to his knees. At least from that position, he could see Heather's twisted form.

"Dear God, no," he croaked, as he crawled fifteen

feet to her side. He could muster no other prayer. As he closed the gap between them, he saw the way her singed shirt smoked over her soot-blackened arm.

Breathing heavily by the time he arrived at her side, he sank to the ground by her head, and put his hands on either side of her face.

"Heather, can you hear me?" His thumbs massaged her cheeks, as he leaned closer. With two fingers he checked the pulse on her neck, which beat a steady cadence. Her chest rose and fell in shallow breaths, and he shook her shoulders gently. "Come on, Sloan. I can't solve this case without you. I need you."

And he did need her. More than he wanted to admit.

She'd become a staple in his life, a fixture that made him smile more than he had in over five years. Smart and sassy, she forced him to think through clues and didn't let him get by with anything less than his all.

And when he was around her, he didn't want to give anything less than that.

He wanted to safeguard her. He just wasn't able to.

As if Reena's memory wasn't enough, he'd proven to Heather three times already that he couldn't protect her. At the hospital, he'd let the man who tried to give her an overdose slip through his fingers. At her home the other night, he'd missed the man hiding in the dark. And now he'd let her get injured by a car bomb.

She deserved better than whatever he could give her. He wasn't enough to keep her safe.

Would he ever be enough?

Her lips were the only part of her that moved when Heather whispered, "You smell like smoke."

Jeremy's chortle didn't surprise either of them. "I think that's you, actually."

"Figures," she mumbled.

"Where you do hurt?"

She sighed. "Everywhere." Finally she flopped her right hand onto her stomach and winced when it landed. "I think there's something wrong with my arm, but if it's okay, I'm not going to look at it right now."

She couldn't see his bittersweet smile, as he looked around at the bystanders. There were nearly a dozen of them now, most on their cell phones, making their way slowly toward the couple on the ground.

He held up his hand to ward them off. Heather would hate looking this weak in front of all her neighbors. "Did someone call an ambulance?" Three women raised their phones in response, and he nodded his thanks.

As he stretched out on his back next to Heather, she curled into his side, tucking her head into his shoulder. He brushed away a strand of her hair that had escaped from her braid and rubbed at a gray spot on her cheek with this thumb.

Beneath the ash and smoke she still smelled like her coconut shampoo, and he wanted to wrap her in his arms and take her away from this entire nightmare.

Heavenly Father, let me figure out a way to keep her safe. I've not done a very good job of it, but I can't deny that I really care about her. Please, don't let me lose her like I did Reena.

"I'm sorry," she mumbled.

"Don't be." He ran his hand down the arm that wasn't injured. He just couldn't stop touching her.

With her eyes still closed, she pressed a soft kiss into the shoulder of his T-shirt. "I don't know why I was so angry, but I…" She coughed from somewhere deep in her lungs. "I'm just sorry."

Sirens sounded somewhere along the freeway. It

would only be minutes until they arrived, so Jeremy held Heather a little closer. She lifted her face from his neck, and he glanced around at the people holding their phones and the group that had made their way to the burning SUV. With his arm around her, they had just enough privacy.

Ducking his head, he pressed his lips to hers.

Unlike the fireworks of their first kiss, this one was soft and gentle, filled with soothing comfort and exactly what they both needed. She leaned in closer to him, and he savored the moment. Just then he could offer her what she needed, a respite from the nightmare of being so ardently pursued.

Just before the police arrived, he pulled back to see the small smile painted on her face.

Gripping the stomach of his T-shirt, she whispered, "You won't go anywhere, will you?"

"I'm with you," he replied just before the police officers descended, bombarding them with questions.

"What happened? Are you all right? How badly are you injured?" asked a baby-faced man in the light blue uniform shirt of the Portland P.D.

Instead of responding to the rapid-fire questions, Jeremy decided to make introductions. Pointing his thumb toward himself, he said, "Jeremy Latham. Sheriff's department." Then he twisted his thumb toward Heather. "Special Agent Heather Sloan with the FBI. Her car was rigged with an explosive."

The officer nodded earnestly. "The fire department is on its way. Paramedics are right behind me. Are you bleeding?"

Jeremy shook his head. "I don't think so. Heather?"

"My arms burn. But I think it's because they're… burned."

"Yes, ma'am."

The poor kid had to have been a rookie as he stood all the way up, hands resting on his belt, looking around. His partner seemed to be herding neighbors away from the fire and directing the ambulance into a spot that wouldn't block the fire truck's entrance.

When the uniformed paramedics arrived, they practically pushed the young officer out of the way, assessing Jeremy and Heather.

The middle-aged blond woman looked at Heather's arms. "We're going to need another ambulance down here."

"I'm going with her," Jeremy said.

"Sir, you really should have your own transport."

"No, thanks. I'll ride with her." This time his tone brooked no argument, so the medics prepped Heather, rolling her onto the stretcher and carrying her away.

Jeremy moved to follow them, but his leg buckled when he tried to stand. Sitting on the grass, he waited for the burly male medic to come back to help him.

Glaring at the white bandages covering both of her forearms, Heather cringed at the memory of the red blisters that had been treated and covered to keep infection from growing there.

"Take these," said the nurse, handing her a plastic cup holding two white pills that looked like aspirin. Heather obeyed, following them with a swig of water. As she set the water down on the table beside the bed in the E.R., she flexed her hands, once again thankful that the car bomb hadn't burned her hands.

She'd had it with the slime that was hunting her.

The nurse stared at the flashing monitor next to the bed then wrote something down. "You're really very lucky," she said, flipping her hair over her shoulder. "You only received second degree burns, and even those aren't as severe as some I've seen."

"Sure." Heather couldn't hold back the sarcasm as she tugged on the shoulder of her flimsy hospital gown. "Someone blew up my car and is trying to kill me, and I'm the lucky one."

The nurse's hazel eyes turned huge in her mousy face, and she stuttered, "I—I'm s-sorry. I didn't know." She backed out of the curtain partition and disappeared.

Heather hung her chin to her chest, shoulders hunched, as she cradled her arms against her stomach.

Lord, I am sorry for snapping at her. But why is all of this happening to me now, right when I feel so far removed from You? It's just that ever since the crash... I don't know. I have to find Kit's killer. I have to. I think that's what You want from me. And I sure know that I won't have any peace until I find him and make sure that justice is served. You gave me this desire for law enforcement, after all. That's how I ended up in the FBI. You must want me to use it now. Right?

"Hey, you." Jeremy's unannounced entrance made her jump, but she quickly recovered, offering him a pained grin at his odd getup. He wore the traditional white hospital gown over his broad shoulders, but his legs were still covered in the blackened jeans he'd been wearing that morning. "How're you feeling?"

She shrugged. "All right. You?"

He covered his mouth with his hand, as a hoarse cough shook his shoulders. "I'm supposed to be breathing pure O2. Apparently your lungs aren't made for breathing smoke."

She shot him the smile she knew he was hoping for. "Any burns?"

"Singed off my arm hair, and a little first degree on my arm, here." He pointed to the gauze-covered spot just below his elbow. How about you?"

She held up both arms. "Second degree burns, but the nurse says they're pretty minor. Aren't I lucky?"

He sat down on the bed next to her, putting his arm around her back, so her only option seemed to be resting her head on his shoulder. "Do they hurt?"

"Yes." She sighed.

"Well, that's good. The doctor told me that really serious burns will injure the nerves so badly that you can't feel anything for a while."

"Well, rest assured. I'm in significant pain, and all they gave me was some over-the-counter painkiller. I kind of miss the morphine drip at Immanuel Lutheran after my knee surgery. I didn't feel much for days."

She could feel his cheeks moving into a smile as he leaned into her hair. "How's your knee?"

"Fine. The doctor X-rayed it, and I didn't tear anything in it. She said I may be a little sore for a couple days, but I should just keep doing my physical therapy."

He nodded and squeezed her a little closer. "Heather?"

"Hmm?"

He paused for a long time, and what she could see of his jeans-clad leg seemed to be flexed with tension. "We need to call Nate."

"No."

"We're out of options. We can't find Mick Gordon—if that's even his real name. You're injured. Again."

"I'm just fine." She twisted to glare directly into his eyes. How dare he imply that she wasn't ready to continue this investigation? "I am completely capable of solving this case."

"Listen to me, Heather. We have nothing more to look into. Everything is a dead end. I just checked with the hospital, and Clay never came back last night. Geoff's lawyer got him out this morning, and he's definitely not talking. We can't figure out Kit's notes. We need to broaden our search base."

With considerable pain in her arms, Heather pushed herself off the bed and maneuvered to the opposite side of the mattress so that Jeremy had to stand as well.

"I'm not having this conversation with you here," she said, waving the flimsy sheet partition at him. "But this discussion is not over."

His forehead wrinkled as his eyes narrowed to slits. "Fine." He spun and strode toward his own room.

The ride back to Heather's house after they'd both been discharged was marked by a pregnant silence. The cabdriver tried to make casual conversation, but the curt responses from the steaming couple in the back was enough to discourage further attempts.

As Jeremy paid the cabbie, Heather ambled toward her front door. A glance over her shoulder confirmed that her designated parking spot was now empty. The police had picked up her car, probably to see if there was evidence that would lead to the bomber.

But who would it lead to?

Who could have planted it when Jeremy's friend had been parked outside her house the entire afternoon and evening before?

"Jeremy?" she called absently over her shoulder as she stared into a rare cloudless sky.

"I'm not in the mood to argue about this right now." He sighed, walking several paces behind her. "Can we talk about something else?"

"I'm not thinking about that." She dismissed their heated discussion earlier with a wave of her hand.

"What's on your mind?" he asked, jogging to catch up with her.

"Why would someone put a bomb in my car? I can't drive." She gestured to her knee brace.

He looked to the empty parking spot, then back at her, shaking his head. "I don't know."

She squinted up at him, letting the spring breeze blow her hair off her neck. "Either they put the bomb in my car before the crash, or they didn't know I can't drive."

An unexpected chill made her shoulders shake, and the trembling only got worse at his reply.

"Or they've decided they don't want you dead quite yet."

FIFTEEN

"I'm going to call Tony and see if he has any information on Clay's disappearance," Jeremy said as he picked up his phone and stalked through the living room. "I'm sure the hospital reported him as a missing person. Maybe they have a lead."

For the first time since they'd arrived back at her house, Heather realized that Jeremy's gait had a noticeable limp.

"What's wrong with your leg?" she called as he reached the front door. He shrugged and pointed to his cell phone as he stepped outside.

She glared at his back as he disappeared, then sank farther into the couch, resting her elbows on her thighs and her chin in her hands. This investigation was not working out the way it was supposed to. At all.

Jeremy clearly hadn't told her about his leg injury, and she might have exaggerated her own perfect health to him at the hospital. At the rate they were collecting injuries, if the case dragged on even another day, they might not even be able to stand at that point.

She had to bring this to a close, without injuring herself or Jeremy further.

And she had to make sure that Kit's killer was brought to justice.

She didn't even look at the screen on her phone when it vibrated on the end table. "Hello." She sighed.

"Heather? It's Nora. Is everything okay?"

What did she know? Had Nate somehow found out about the explosion?

"Why do you ask?"

"You just sounded tired. Have you been pushing yourself too hard? Too much physical therapy?"

Heather kept this sigh silent. "Not at all."

"Oh. Well, I came by yesterday and you weren't there." Nora paused, sounding insecure for the first time since Heather had met her. "I mean, I know you told me not to come by, but I haven't heard from you in a few days. I was worried about you."

She ran a hand through her tangled curls, then eyed the black smudges where the once white bandages on her arms had taken the soot from her clothes. The dirt had likely transferred to her face as well. She probably looked as bad as she felt.

"I'm sorry. I was out...running errands with Jeremy."

"Jeremy? The sheriff's deputy?"

Oh, great. Now she'd done it. She'd opened up the can of worms about her personal life, and Nora was just the girl to dig into it. She didn't even wait for Heather's response. "You've been spending a lot of time with each other, haven't you?" Her voice turned light with a teasing lilt. "Is there something going on between you? You know Nate will have to check him out, as your official older-brother-type."

Heather gave the obligatory chortle, but her stomach flipped. Nora may have been teasing, but Nate certainly wouldn't be when he found out how much time she'd been spending with the deputy. And how much her feelings for him had developed in such a short amount of time.

"I'm sure that won't be necessary," Heather said.

"Of course, I'm kidding. I'm sure you and Jeremy are just friends."

Right. Just friends. Practically partners. And completely platonic.

The image of their first kiss and the repeat in the grass that morning flashed across her mind, sending the butterflies in her middle into overdrive.

Maybe not.

"Has he been helping you run errands and get groceries and things?"

"Who?" Heather's cheeks flushed warm as she was dragged from a quite pleasant memory.

Nora laughed again. "I think you need to get more sleep. You sound a little out of things."

"Right. I haven't been sleeping very well."

Nora paused again, hesitancy returning to the tone of her voice. "Heather, I know we've only known each other for a couple of months, but if you ever want to talk about what you're going through—with losing your sister and all—I'm here, and I know how to listen."

"Thank you." Heather looked down at her feet. "I appreciate it. I really do. I'm just not ready to talk about it." And she wouldn't be until the killer was caught and shipped off for life.

"All right. Well, I'll let you try to get some sleep, but please do call me if you need anything. I can run errands for you or anything."

"Thanks, Nora. I'll call if I think of something."

She hung up just as Jeremy walked back inside, a

dusting of sweat lining his top lip, reflecting the over-head light. He cocked his head to the side, asking his question without speaking.

And the traitorous butterflies returned.

She looked away from him, hoping she'd be able to concentrate if she wasn't watching to see when the wave of hair on his forehead would bounce or if the muscles in his neck flexed when he spoke.

"Nora called. She stopped by yesterday, and I wasn't here. She was worried."

"Did you tell her about the car bomb?"

Heather shook her head. "It didn't come up."

He put his hands on his hips and stared at the ground between his shoes. He didn't look at her either, and with a pang in her chest, she hoped it was for the same reason she was having a hard time looking at him.

"Heather, we have to talk about this."

"What did Tony say?" she asked, dodging the dreaded conversation yet again.

"Nothing new." Jeremy ran his hand through his hair, finally managing to look at her for more than two sec-onds consecutively. "No sign of Clay. And it looks like PNW has shut down. Geoff and Newt Martinson seem to have disappeared, too."

"Do you think they have Clay?"

Jeremy shrugged. "It's certainly possible." His gaze moved and stayed right over her shoulder, and she didn't mind not having the weight of it directly on her. "We're still in deep."

"I know." She steepled her fingers and rested the tip of her nose on them. Her insides felt like knots. As long as the killer hadn't finished the job, her very life put Jeremy in danger. The person behind the drugs and the crash wanted her.

But maybe he wanted her alive, if the timing of the car bomb was an indicator.

"What if he wants me alive?" she said, breaking the silence. "What if he wants me?"

"We'll find him before he gets to you. I promise, Heather." Those words seemed to cause him pain, but she pushed on.

She toyed with an idea, rolling it over and over in her mind. Finally she said, "I could draw him out."

Jeremy nearly choked as a hacking cough tore from his throat.

She looked up at him, standing on the other side of the room. This time their eyes met, their gazes locked. She tried to smile at him, but his face turned pale and he wiped his upper lip with the back of his hand.

"You're kidding, right?" he croaked.

"This could work."

"What are you talking about? You want to set yourself out there as some kind of bait to trap this guy?"

She nodded slowly. "The longer we wait, the more banged up we're going to get. He's destroying our ability to fight back, and soon we won't have the strength to do it at all."

"That's ridiculous. You're practically still on crutches."

"No, I'm not. I'm walking just fine."

He continued, ignoring her completely. "Your arms are burned, and you haven't had a decent night's sleep since the crash. You couldn't even walk around the clearing two days ago."

She stood, needing to pace as much as her tender knee would allow, also needing to show Jeremy just how wrong he was about her current abilities.

"So...what? You're just going to stand out on the street and hope he comes to find you?" A muscle in his jaw jumped, and the vein in his forehead throbbed in a rapid beat. "Good plan."

She rolled her eyes to keep from slugging him in the arm. "I'll figure something out. I'll spread the word about where I'm going to be, and then we'll ambush him. You'll be there to back me up." She took a deep, steadying breath. "Right?"

"No way. I'm not playing a part in helping you get yourself killed." He grabbed the back of the recliner in front of him and leaned into it, like he'd fall over without it. "We need to call Nate or someone else at the Bureau."

"No. It's not an option."

"Be reasonable, Heather. We need help, and you're an FBI agent."

"An agent who's on medical leave and was ordered to not get involved in this case. Don't you realize that this could mean my job?"

He jammed both hands into his hair and looked like he was going to pull it out by the roots. She felt like doing the same.

How could someone give her butterflies one minute, and make her so angry the next?

Jeremy seemed to have the code to all of her buttons and was ready and willing to press them to get whatever he wanted.

"We can explain this to Nate. He'll understand. He wants to protect you."

"What if the sheriff told you to stop investigating a case and to take mandatory leave? What would happen if you didn't listen?"

His broad shoulders hunched as he shoved his hands into his pockets. "I don't know." He groaned and pinched his nose. "I guess I'd be investigated for insubordination and possibly obstruction of justice."

"And?"

He hung his head. "And my job would be on the line."

"You see, then. I can't go to Nate."

"Then let me go to him, alone. He doesn't have to know that you're even involved in this investigation." His eyes suddenly glowed. "This'll work! I'll get any information that the Bureau has, and then I can get this case wrapped up."

Heather sagged against the sofa as though it were a lifeline. "So you're going to leave me out of my own investigation?"

"No. That's not it at all." He stepped toward her, reaching out to touch her.

"Don't even think about it," she seethed, jerking out of his reach.

"Heather, help me understand." He took another step toward her, closing the gap between them to less than two feet. His voice remained calm and soothing, and it grated on her raw nerves. How could he keep it together when she wanted to fly apart over this whole mess? "Please, I just want to do what's best for us. We can solve this case without you having to put yourself at risk."

"But what if Nate can't help us? What if the Bureau doesn't have any useful information?"

"Then we'll be right where we are now." He rubbed the back of his neck. "Would that be so bad?"

Her eyes burned in anger, and she rubbed them, trying to force the moisture back. "What if one wasted day is too much? What if by this time tomorrow, you've been seriously injured—or worse—by this lunatic? I can't let him take anyone else away from me. He needs to be caught, so he can be held accountable for his crimes."

He shook his head, clearly at a loss.

"I have to find him. I have to make sure that he's punished for what he did to Kit. She deserves justice."

Jeremy nodded slowly, rubbing open palms down the sides of his jeans. "Are you sure it's justice that you want?" He inhaled quickly, continuing before she could gather a response, "I just mean you've seemed pretty intent on finding this guy from the beginning. And I certainly don't blame you. He's taken a lot from you and tried to kill you several times, but it seems to me that maybe you're after more than just seeing justice served."

Her head snapped back. "Of course justice is what I'm after. What else would I want?" Her breathing turned shallow, as she glared across the room at the man who usually sent her heart racing. Now he sent her blood boiling.

He looked away, scratching at the back of his neck. When his gaze returned to meet hers, he said, "Are you sure you're not after revenge?"

"That's—that's ludicrous." Her knee throbbed and she wanted to sit down, but she couldn't give him the upper hand in this argument by taking the lower ground. "He deserves to be punished, and it's my job to make sure that happens. That's all."

"But it's not your job. Not this time." He held up his hand, and she bit down on the retort on the tip of her tongue. "You're supposed to be recovering and recuperating. This isn't your case to investigate. This time it's not your job. It's personal."

"So what if it is?"

"You're putting your own life on the line to capture

this guy because you think you owe it to Kit. But you don't have to. Don't you see?"

His eyes turned hard, and she couldn't read anything there except a flicker of pain. What could possibly be causing him so much pain that it flashed across his face? He'd been limping earlier, but he didn't seem to have a problem standing at the moment.

When Heather didn't say anything, he spoke again. "Can't you trust that God will take care of this? Don't you think He'll see justice served?"

"Are you really that naive?" she spat. "Sometimes the bad guys go free."

"I know that." He sighed, his shoulders sagging. "But I'm not saying the justice system is always perfect. I am saying that God is in control. You have to turn this over to Him, instead of letting this case consume you."

Her eyes narrowed, and she wanted to jab back at him. She couldn't hold back the retaliatory barb. "Oh, that's rich coming from someone who still thinks he's responsible for his fiancée's death. Someone who just let her die and is now only using my sister's death to ease his own conscience."

When the words were out there, hanging like laundry on the line, she clapped her hands over her mouth, her eyes suddenly filling with tears. She tried to pull them back in, but they couldn't be taken back. And she couldn't manage to say anything that would even begin to make up for that terrible accusation.

Jeremy's eyebrows pinched together, and his face lost its color. Through pinched lips, he managed, "All right. Clearly I'm not going to be able to talk you out of doing this, so go ahead and do it. But don't expect me to watch you put your neck on the line."

He spun and marched toward the front door. There

he turned to look at Heather, tears leaking down her cheeks. "Try to be careful, all right?"

She nodded. Then he was gone.

And she could only manage to sink to the floor, aching with the grief over the horrible things she'd said, the death of her sister, the uncertainty of her future.

And the loss of the man she loved, at her own hand.

SIXTEEN

Heather needed a plan.

But after a sleepless night of playing the scene with Jeremy over and over in her mind, she was no closer to figuring out how to flush the perp into the open, make an arrest and avenge Kit's murder than she had been a week before, while lying in a hospital bed. Still, at least she was mobile now.

Her weak knee trembled and nearly gave out completely as she fell into the counter.

Well, mostly mobile.

She nursed her favorite mug filled with coffee as she settled into a chair at the table. Kit's notes on the case were strewn across the top, and she flipped two pages over, scanning for anything that might be the clue to break the case.

Of course, it was useless.

She'd been over these notes a hundred times in her mind, and every time she ended up in the same place. Absolutely nowhere.

There was only the disappeared Mick Gordon. And the elusive Mr. F. Or maybe Mrs. F. Either way, Heather was no closer to figuring out who F might be.

Mick had had a phone number, but F didn't. Was that

because Kit knew him, and didn't need to write down his number?

Unlikely.

Heather plunged her fingers into her freshly washed hair and rubbed her scalp, hoping to stimulate a brilliant idea. Or maybe just forget the miserable argument she'd had with Jeremy the night before.

Don't think about him. Think about Kit.

It had become her mantra to get through the night. It wasn't working very well, but she was trying.

"How do I draw out the person who wants me dead?" she asked the empty chair across from her. "Stand on the street corner and hope he drives by?" She heaved a loud sigh. "Nope. That's not going to work."

She rolled her neck several times and pulled the lapels of her fuzzy, green robe closer to her chin.

"Who might get word to him without it sounding like I'm trying to draw him out?"

Nothing. Nothing. And then suddenly the seed of an idea.

Slowly she picked up her phone and called the sheriff's office. "May I speak with Deputy Gonzales, please?" The young deputy who'd guarded her for Jeremy was her best first step.

"One moment, please," said the receptionist on the other end of the line.

While the line lay silent for several seconds, she tried not to wonder if Jeremy was there, sitting at his desk, maybe seeing a blinking light on his phone.

"This is Gonzales."

"Hi." Her throat suddenly felt full and she cleared it loudly. "This is Heather Sloan. Do you remember me?"

"Um, of course, Ms. Sloan," said the younger man.

He had a distinct way of making her feel old. "Is there something you need? Latham isn't in this morning."

Her hand holding the phone shook slightly, so she tucked the phone between her ear and shoulder and clasped her hands on the table. "I was calling to speak with you, actually."

"You were?" He sounded confused, and so young.

"Yes. Do you remember the man that Jeremy—I mean, Deputy Latham—booked, named Geoff Conner?"

"Yes, ma'am."

"Could you possibly tell me who his lawyer is?"

He didn't speak for what felt like ages. "Latham said that I shouldn't give you any information."

That rat!

How had he known she'd go to Gonzales?

Smiling and hoping he could hear it in her voice, she said, "Please. I just wanted to check into a few things with the lawyer. You know Geoff was outside my home when he and Latham got into that fight, right? Since he's been released, I just want to know if he's still in the area."

"I suppose that would be okay. Just a second." He put the phone down and she heard papers rustling. When he picked it back up, he said, "The lawyer that came in and bailed him out was Lee Cooper."

Tempted to ask for the lawyer's phone number, she opened her mouth, then closed it quickly. "Thank you, Deputy Gonzales. You've been very helpful."

"My pleasure, ma'am. And if you wouldn't mind, please don't mention to Latham that you got the name from me."

"Of course not," she said before hanging up.

Quickly looking up the number for the lawyer, Heather called his office.

"Cooper, Cooper and Grabalski. How may I direct your call?" said a nasal voice on the other end.

"Lee Cooper, please," Heather said in her most authoritative tone. "This is urgent."

"Are you a client of Mr. Cooper?"

"This is Special Agent Sloan with the FBI."

"One moment, Ms. Sloan."

Heather held her breath as she waited. Her plan just might work. If only Lee Cooper was connected to the person she assumed he was and would do what she expected him to.

"Special Agent Sloan." His voice was slick and bred for the courtroom. "What can I do for you today?"

"Mr. Cooper." Her chest rose and fell faster than she wanted to admit, and she wrapped her freshly bandaged arms around her middle. "Mr. Cooper, I'd like to set up a meeting with one of your clients."

"Really? Which one?"

Like he didn't know. "Geoff Conner."

"Agent Sloan, you must know that I wouldn't recommend my client meet with you without being present myself." He sounded like a scolding uncle. "But if you'd like to set up something in my office, we might be able to arrange that."

"I was actually thinking about Fernhill Park."

"Why would my client want to meet you in the park?"

"Would you just pass this message along to Geoff? I think I can help him out with his situation with the sheriff, and I'll be at the grove of trees near northeast Ainsworth Street this afternoon at five-thirty. He'll be there if he wants my help."

When she hung up, Heather thought she might be sick to her stomach. She stared at the black phone lying on the table, desperately wanting to call Jeremy but refusing to give in to the urge.

He wouldn't want to talk with her anyway. Not after what she'd said to him.

In his shoes, she wouldn't forgive her, either.

Right now she just needed to focus on getting through the day and getting ready to meet the person calling the shots. If she wasn't mistaken, Geoff Conner couldn't afford a lawyer like Lee Cooper. He was probably being paid by whoever had sent Geoff.

Whoever had made that chopper crash.

And a lawyer like Cooper passed along news of FBI agents alone in a park. Immediately.

Jeremy hit the snooze button on his alarm for what felt like the tenth time. He let his arm flop over his eyes to block out the morning light coming through the window in his bedroom.

His stomach clenched when he realized that he was indeed back in his own bed. While it was nice to stretch out on the king-size mattress, part of him longed for the couch in Heather's living room, even if his feet did hang off the end.

At least there he'd know she was safe, instead of being relegated to worrying about it all the way across town.

Why had he walked out on her?

Sure, her words had stung, but he shouldn't have left her unprotected. He'd acted like a fool five years before when he hadn't spoken up, and he'd given a repeat performance last night. He'd let his emotions get in the way, instead of doing what he needed to in order to care for Heather.

His ego vied for control, reminding him of her barb.

That's rich coming from someone who still thinks he's responsible for his fiancée's death. Someone who just let her die and is now only using my sister's death to ease his own conscience.

She'd said it to hurt him. And it had hit the mark.

But wasn't it at least mostly true?

He'd been lecturing her on trusting that God was in control, but he'd been carrying around the guilt over Reena's death for a long time. And there was certainly part of him that hoped working to solve Kit's death would begin to make amends for his mistakes. Yet beyond that and beyond the simple fact that he'd been assigned the case, there was something more that kept him sleeping on a couch for a week.

A spunky blonde with laser blue eyes.

His cell phone alarm beeped again and he swatted at it, thankful for the distraction that derailed his thoughts from a track he didn't want to be on. Flipping the covers back and rolling out of bed, he eyed his swollen ankle, which he'd twisted when Heather's car had exploded. Better to focus on the physical pain than his wayward emotions.

He glanced at the phone in his hand as he debated calling her. He didn't need another reason to think about her, but he certainly wanted to know that she was okay—that her house hadn't been broken into while he wasn't there.

The phone was dialing before he even made the conscious decision to do so. After several seconds, it went directly to voice mail. "This is Heather Sloan. Sorry I missed you." His stomach clenched just hearing her voice. Was she ignoring his call? Or had something terrible happened?

"It's me. Listen, I'm sorry about yesterday. Will you call me? I'm worried about you. I just need to know you're okay."

He stared at the empty wall across the room, weighing his options for the day. He could look for Clay. More dead ends.

He could try to find Heather. She probably wasn't at home.

If he knew her—and he really did, even if they'd only met a little over a week before—she'd be putting that pigheaded plan of hers into place. She'd have her neck out on the line, maybe by the end of the day.

And there was really only one person Heather feared enough to maybe put a stop to her plan.

He lunged across the room, favoring his right ankle as he hobbled toward the shower.

Ten minutes later, clean and ready to go, he hopped out his front door, staggering toward his car. Once behind the wheel, he didn't hesitate until he arrived at the enormous government building that housed the Portland office of the FBI. Noise from the nearby Riverfront Park along the Willamette River drowned out the pounding of his heart as he looked up into the windows, wondering which Heather would have been sitting behind in better times.

When he reached the fourth floor, he took a deep breath, nodding at the petite receptionist who looked up to greet him.

"May I help you?"

He pulled his badge out of the pocket of his jeans. "Deputy Jeremy Latham. I'm with the sheriff's department. I need to see Nate Andersen."

"Do you have an appointment with him?"

"No."

"Then I'm sorry. He only—"

"Heather Sloan's life is on the line."

Her face turned pale, washed out even under the heavy layer of makeup applied there. "One moment, please." Immediately she picked up the phone, punching in an extension and whispering furiously.

He looked away for a second, and when he turned back a man with dark hair and steel-blue eyes stood in front of him.

"SAC Nate Andersen," he said, holding out his hand. "You are?"

The other man's grip was firm but not intentionally intimidating. "Jeremy Latham. I've been investigating the helicopter crash that killed Kit Sloan."

"You have some information on Heather?"

Jeremy looked around quickly. "Is there somewhere we can speak privately?"

Nate gave him a curt nod and led him to a small conference room down a short hall. He held the glass door open for Jeremy then followed him in, closing the door behind them.

The veins in Nate's neck looked as if they might explode, and he crossed his arms over his chest, neither taking nor offering one of the plush leather chairs. His glare remained hard, but he didn't speak, so Jeremy took his cue.

"Heather has always spoken so highly of you." Nate didn't relax a muscle. "And she'll never speak to me again when she finds out I came here and spoke to you about this, but I don't have any choice. She's determined to do something stupid."

The corner of one of Nate's eyes twitched, and Jeremy

took that as a sign, continuing on, no matter how much he felt like a suitor talking to his girlfriend's father. "We met about a week ago when I was assigned this case and went to the hospital to ask her some questions about the crash." A muscle in Nate's jaw jumped, but he didn't say anything. Jeremy shoved his hands in his pockets, not knowing what else to do with them. "I thought the crash was just an accident until someone tried to kill Heather in the hospital."

Nate's face turned pale and he leaned onto the back of one of the chairs, seeming to need it just to stay upright. "How?"

"A lethal overdose of a new street drug injected into her IV."

"How did I not hear about this?" Nate's voice turned thick with emotion, and it was obvious that he cared very much for Heather. But for some reason it didn't make Jeremy's gut squeeze with jealousy like just the mention of Clay did. Nate seemed more like an older brother, not competition for Heather's affections.

Jeremy shrugged. "Heather was adamant about joining in on the investigation, and—"

"What?" Nate exploded, his face going from white to purple and skipping every shade in between as he slammed one fist into an open palm. "I told her to stay out of this investigation. I told her to work on recovering and let you do your job." By the end of his last word, his voice had tapered down to a low growl. "I should have known."

"That's why she wouldn't let me come to you."

"So the two of you have been investigating the crash together for the last week?"

"That's right." Jeremy met the man's hard gaze, but

felt a little sick to his stomach. There was no telling what this might do to Heather's career.

But he didn't have a choice about coming to Nate. Did he?

"And?"

"And we think it all centers on a drug ring."

Nate crossed his arms again. "What makes you say that?"

"Before she died, Kit told Heather to follow the drugs, and when we went to the crash site—" Nate shook his head as though he couldn't believe what he was hearing "—we found cocaine residue on a boulder."

"Any idea who's behind it?"

"No. But we found some notes from Kit the night that Heather's house was broken into."

Nate blinked, clearly still in disbelief. "Someone broke into Heather's house? And she didn't tell me?"

Jeremy had the poise to grimace and apologize. "I'm sorry. She was adamant that you not find out. She's terrified of losing her position here at the Bureau if you found out she was working on the case against your orders. And I think she's afraid that the person responsible for Kit's death is going to go free if she doesn't catch him."

"What's she going to do?"

"She's setting herself out as bait to catch him."

Nate shook his head and nodded toward a chair. "You'd better sit down and tell me everything you know."

Jeremy obliged, sliding into a leather seat across the wide table from Nate, who slumped in his chair. In his crisp black suit, he didn't seem the type to slump, and Jeremy could almost see the weight on his shoulders forcing him into that position.

With as many details as he could, Jeremy replayed every major event of the last week. From the attempt on Heather's life at the hospital, to the words scrawled across her front door, to Jeremy's brawl with Geoff, to Clay's disappearance and finally to the car bomb.

Nate scrubbed his hands over his face, his features strained and his five o'clock shadow the only color on his face. "She's out there right now because she thinks Clay has been abducted." He shook his head as he looked back up at Jeremy. "She thinks that he's in danger because of her?"

"Something like that."

"How could someone so brilliant do something so stupid?"

Jeremy nodded, understanding Nate's point, but still needing to speak up for Heather. "She's scared. She's just lost her sister, a madman has been hunting her and she's desperate to see it resolved without anyone else she loves being put in danger." He wiped his hands on his jeans, then squeezed them into fists. "I think she thinks putting herself out there, where he can grab her, will bring a quick end to this nightmare."

Nate eyed Jeremy out of the corner of his eye. "Well, clearly you don't agree with her, or you wouldn't be here."

Jeremy shook his head. "Of course not."

"Then why are you here?"

Jeremy didn't blink, looking straight into the other man's hard gaze. He longed to tell the whole truth— that he had fallen in love with Heather and that he just wanted to see her safe and protected. By someone who could do that without fail.

Instead he offered facts. "We think Kit was investigating the drug ring that's responsible for this whole ordeal. She left Heather some notes, but they're pretty cryptic."

"Was she getting too close, so they took her out?"

"Most likely."

"But then why go after Heather? Or Clay, for that matter?"

Jeremy bit his bottom lip. "My best guess? Whoever's behind this doesn't know how much Kit might have spilled."

Nate rubbed his temples in slow circles. "All right. Where is Heather now?"

"I don't know." Jeremy cringed having to admit it. Nate didn't say anything, just quirked one eyebrow, and Jeremy felt obliged to confess. "We had a fight last night, and she won't pick up my calls."

Nate immediately pulled his phone from his suit's breast pocket, calling Heather with a single button push. He shook his head. "Straight to voice mail." His forehead wrinkled, and Jeremy wondered if that was the extent of emotion he would reveal. "You didn't answer my question a minute ago. Why are you here? What do you think I can do?"

"Can you help me find someone mentioned in Kit's notes? I think he might be the key to finding out who's responsible for all of this. We've tried to track him down, but he's not in any city or state databases." Jeremy laid his hand on his bouncing knee, trying to keep it still, but the tension in his muscles wouldn't dissipate. "If I can find the man behind all of this mess before he finds Heather, I can protect her."

Nate shot out of his chair, motioning for Jeremy to follow him. "Let's go check some databases. What's his name?"

"Mick Gordon."

Nate stopped, his hand on the door handle, his eyebrows raised. "There's a reason you didn't find him in your databases. He's an FBI informant."

SEVENTEEN

The little man behind the chained door quaked as Jeremy took a menacing step toward him. "Are you Mick Gordon?"

"Shh." He brought a shaking finger to his lips, his eyes bright. "What do you want?"

"Tell me what you know about Kit Sloan."

Already gray features turned white, and Mick's trembling hand on the door rattled the security chain. "I don't know anyone by that name."

Nate had warned Jeremy that Gordon wasn't the sharpest, but he had good information. As a career petty criminal, he managed to have his nose in just enough of everyone's business to be both useful and a threat. But Nate had assured him that Gordon would cooperate with an intimidating presence.

"You told my partner that something you said got Kit killed. Tell me what it was."

"I never talked to your partner."

Jeremy's eyes turned to slits. "On the phone, three days ago. You were quite rude and hung up on us."

Gordon's shoulders twitched as he shook his head. "It—it wasn't me. I—I never talked to her."

Jeremy leaned his shoulder into the door. "I never said

my partner is a woman." Gordon tried to slam the rotting wood that had probably been new when the apartment was built thirty years before, but it didn't budge against Jeremy's foot wedged at the base. "I want answers, and I want them now."

The smaller man chewed on a fingernail, cowering back from the door. It wouldn't take much force to pop the chain and push the door open, but Jeremy hoped the informant would make good on his role and start talking once he realized Jeremy meant business.

Finally, Gordon sagged into the wall, his face crumpling. "I never meant for her to get hurt. But she called and asked. And I didn't know—I didn't think that something like this would happen." He sniffled loudly.

Jeremy rested his fist a foot from Gordon's face, the muscles in his jaw working overtime. "Tell me exactly what you told her."

"I told her that I used to work for this guy, delivering packages and stuff. I didn't know what was in them, but it was good money."

"Drugs?"

He shrugged. "Like I said, I didn't know what was in them. I didn't *want* to know. She wanted to know if I'd recognize anyone I dropped off for. She showed me a couple pictures and I didn't know them."

"Get to the point," Jeremy growled. He didn't have time to waste. Not when Heather was anywhere but next to him, probably putting herself in harm's way.

"She showed me one. A picture. Of her and this guy. And I knew the guy. He was the one who hired me. He paid good."

"Kit was in the picture with the guy?"

"Yes."

Jeremy thought his head might explode from the

pressure caused by waiting on the guy to just spill the information. When it became apparent he wasn't going to say more, Jeremy prompted him. "And? Do you remember his name? Or Kit's reaction?"

"She…she looked sad at first. Then mad."

Jeremy pressed his palm against his forehead. "What was his name?"

"Clay."

"Clay Kramer?" All the pieces of the puzzle clicked into place in an instant. This was why Kit's notes had been so cryptic, why she'd tried to hide what she was investigating—she'd figured out that her own fiancé was running a drug ring. That's what the "F" had stood for—fiancé.

Jeremy spun around before Gordon had even finished nodding his head, his stomach dropping to the bottom of his shoes. Sailing across the lawn to his car, he ignored everything but the need to get to Heather.

She wouldn't know to be on her guard against Clay. She would just be happy to see him and a cinch to disarm.

She would be an easy mark for her sister's fiancé.

If he didn't get to her first.

He peeled out of the parking lot before the car door even closed behind him.

Snatching the phone from his pocket, he pressed a single button to reach Heather, but her cell went straight to voice mail.

"Heather, it's Clay! He's the one! He's behind everything! Call me back as soon as you get this! Let me know that you're all right." As soon as he hung up, the phone vibrated, indicating an incoming call. "Heather?"

"Um…no. It's Tony."

Jeremy sagged into the seat of his car, steering around

a trash can along the side of the road. He had to get to Heather in time. He just had to.

But he didn't even know where she was.

Braking at a stop sign, he considered which turn to make. Would she still be home? Had she gone to the PNW office? Or had she decided she needed help and gone looking for him?

Doubtful on the last two options, he turned toward her town house, pushing the engine hard.

"Jeremy, you still there?"

"Yeah, I'm here, Tony. What's going on?"

Tony sighed. "I heard something about Heather today. I knew you'd want to know right away."

Jeremy's grip on the wheel nearly cut off circulation to his fingers. "What'd you hear?"

"One of the other guys brought in a guy who was spouting off stuff about how a lawyer paid him to take a message to his boss about an FBI agent being in the park tonight at sunset for a meeting."

"Did he call her by name?"

"No, but he's been mumbling about how she's going to get what her sister got."

"What park?" Jeremy demanded. He squinted into the setting sun, his mind racing but not finding a plan to settle on.

Tony's voice, which usually passed for a pretty good James Earl Jones impression, turned soft. "I don't know. The perp wouldn't say. He passed out drunk before we could get any more info out of him. I have him in lockup, but he's useless now."

"How many parks are there in the city?"

"There has to be at least a dozen just this side of the 205."

Jeremy slammed his fist against the steering wheel.

He had just minutes to figure out what park she'd be at, but where could he possibly start?

Still speeding toward her house, he swerved to the shoulder, pulling to a stop. He didn't have time to waste going in the wrong direction.

"What can I do, man?" Tony finally asked.

"Put out an APB on her. And one on Clay Kramer."

"Kramer? As in..."

"Kit's fiancé...and I think he's the one Heather is about to meet in the park. She just doesn't know it."

After several long moments, Tony groaned. "This is going to get messy. What else can I do?"

"Pray."

"Done."

Immediately after ending the call with Tony, Jeremy dialed Nate on his personal cell phone, which he'd given to Jeremy before sending him off to meet Gordon.

"Jeremy? Have you talked to Heather? She's still not answering her phone."

"No. But I just talked to a buddy at the P.D. He has info that Heather set up a meeting with our guy at a park tonight at sunset."

Nate's voice sounded thick. "But it's after five already. Are you headed to the park?"

"I don't know which one." Jeremy rubbed his hand over his hair. He wanted to pull it all out, but he mustered the energy to refrain. Finding and protecting Heather. That was most important.

Through the phone a chair creaked and Nate hollered to someone else. "Myles! You remember when Heather took care of Kenzie's dog, Henry?" There was a short pause. "Didn't she take him to a park?"

The other voice sounded distant, but Jeremy could still make out his words. "Sure. She took him to Fernhill.

I think it was near her sister's place, and they met there a few times. Why?"

Nate's voice came clearly back on the line. "You get that?"

"It's worth a chance." Jeremy peeled out, pulling into traffic and pulling a one-eighty at the nearest light.

Sailing down the road, lights flashing and siren going, Jeremy prayed like he had never prayed before.

"God, please let me get to her in time. Please let her be at Fernhill Park, and let me get there before anything else happens to her. Don't let this be like…"

His voice cracked, and he couldn't continue the words that he wanted and needed to say. He needed to admit how long he'd carried the weight of shame and regret over the loss of Reena and his other friends. He needed to put a voice to the fear that had kept him from realizing the true depth of his attraction for the special agent who had taken over his life the last week.

But as the buildings flew by in a blur, he could only think about the last words Heather had spoken to him. She'd told him he was doing exactly what he'd accused her of. He'd refused to give control to God, wielding the responsibility for something that wasn't in his control.

"Heavenly Father, Heather's right. I thought I could have and should have protected Reena, and I should have spoken up. But I wasn't in control of anything that day. You were."

He heaved a loud sigh as the bottom of the sun slipped below the horizon in his rearview mirror. "We're running out of time, but I'm trusting You to be in control today, too."

* * *

Heather checked the time on her cell phone again. Two minutes past the time she'd told Lee Cooper that she'd be in the park and another two missed calls— one from Jeremy and one from Nate. The last of Jeremy's messages that she'd listened to had been an hour earlier.

"Call me right away, Sloan. Get home immediately. Just check in with me!" he'd yelled. After a short pause in a defeated voice, "Heather, I'm sorry for the way we left things, but I'm going crazy with worry here. Nate got me a way to find Mick Gordon, and I'm heading to his place right now. So just…don't do anything stupid. I need to know that you're okay."

Pushing away all thoughts of the two men and possibly the loss of her job she'd have to face after this, she thought about the lawyer who she'd been certain would pass the information along to his client. This was still the best idea she had. In mere minutes she could know the identity of her sister's killer and make sure he got what he deserved.

She rubbed her hand across the waistband at the back of her jeans, confirming that her service weapon still rested beneath her light jacket.

The sun wasn't quite gone yet, but the park was beginning to clear out.

A breaking stick behind her made her jump, and she turned around as fast as she could, while leaning heavily on her crutches. A little brown dog barked at her, then picked up the stick he'd been chewing on and trotted off.

Her heart didn't calm down as fast as the dog disappeared, and she rubbed her palms on the foam handles of the crutches. She didn't really need them anymore, but it wouldn't hurt for her to have a little secret when this went down.

If it went down.

She scanned the faces of the people wandering on the other side of the park, and as it had been a year ago when she'd taken a friend's dog here, this section seemed almost deserted, save for a puppy here or there.

Suddenly she picked out a figure in her peripheral vision walking straight toward her. Turning to look at his familiar strides, she almost rubbed her eyes, not believing who was headed her way.

"Clay! What are you doing here? Are you all right? Where have you been?"

The setting sun was at his back, making it difficult to see his face until he was close enough to reach out to touch her arm with a warm hand. "I'm fine."

She touched the red mark at his hairline where he'd been cut during his attack. "Are you sure you're okay?"

"Of course. Why wouldn't I be?"

She squinted at him, trying to figure out what was wrong with the picture in front of her. Clay looked like he always did, polished and handsome. His khakis and blue dress shirt had been perfectly pressed, his hair meticulously combed into place.

She took a careful step back, her stomach twisting. "Where have you been?"

"Taking care of business." He shrugged as if it was no big deal that he'd just disappeared from the hospital and not been in touch for two days.

"What are you doing here?" Her voice almost cracked, but she kept it together with a concentrated effort.

"I came to see you." His face didn't move, didn't

show any emotion, and Heather took another step back. He mirrored her actions. "I came to see if you're okay. Clearly you still are. And it's high time that situation was remedied."

She swallowed the lump building in her throat, fear boiling in her stomach. "How did you know I was here?"

His lip curled, transforming his features into perfect cruelty.

The truth formed in her gut like a rock, stealing her breath and leaving her head spinning.

"Lee Cooper told you." It wasn't really a question.

"Of course he did. And since no one else could get done what I'd been asking them to do for weeks, I guess I'm going to have to do it myself."

She blinked into brown eyes filled with hatred and wished that she had returned at least one of Jeremy's phone calls.

"You're shaking," Clay taunted, closing the gap between them by another step.

"N-no I'm not," she lied, blinking against the anger mixing with her fear deep in her chest.

"What did you think was going to happen here tonight?" His tone continued mocking her, but his eyes remained cruel, hard as the barrel of her gun pressing against her lower back.

"I thought Kit's killer was going to come, and he has." She sucked in a quick breath, as Clay shrugged one shoulder and carelessly turned his head away for just a moment. She reached behind her back and yanked the gun from its hiding place.

In a fraction of a second, she had Clay's chest lined up with the site at the end of the barrel.

"You're not going to shoot me," he said with a laugh.

"You have too many questions about why all of this has happened and what happened to your sister. I'm the only one with the answers you need."

She shook her head, denying what she knew to be true. She did want answers.

The sun finally set completely, leaving only the park lights to illuminate Clay's arrogant smirk.

The rage inside her churned, and she jabbed her gun at him. "Just give me a reason to."

Suddenly a dog barked right behind her, and she jumped. With incredible speed Clay grabbed the gun with his left hand and wrenched it from her grasp. With his other hand, he produced a black pistol from under his arm.

Heather's vision narrowed, and she couldn't take her gaze off of his weapon as she waited to die by the same hand that had killed Kit.

Only one thought broke through the shock.

She would never see Jeremy again.

God, forgive me for what I said to him. And please help him forgive me for landing myself in this situation…and for dying before I had the chance to tell him I love him.

EIGHTEEN

Heather stood frozen, unable to move or even process the truth she'd just realized. She loved Jeremy—and she was about to die.

"Oh, did you think you'd have the upper hand out here?" Clay mocked, pouting his lower lip. "You weren't expecting me, were you?" His mouth twisted with hatred as he took a menacing step toward her, the gun mere inches from her chest. He couldn't possibly miss a fatal shot at this distance.

With his free hand he gestured to the empty park behind him. "I guess we're all alone now." He cocked his head to the right. "And to think…we were almost relatives."

She closed her eyes and Jeremy's face immediately appeared.

The way his hair fell across his forehead and the way his dark brown eyes glimmered in the early morning. The way he drank nearly solid coffee. The way he held her close and kissed her as though he'd never let anything else ever happen to her. The way he hadn't retaliated when she'd been so terrible to him.

She had to live. She had to make it through this, if only to apologize.

And if she were lucky, maybe more.

Maybe there was a bigger reason for what they had endured. A plan for why they'd been thrown together like this. She squeezed shaking hands into fists, resolve flooding her veins and giving her the strength to open her eyes and look at the whole situation before her.

She swallowed thickly, willing her voice to stay strong. If she could keep him talking, maybe she could stall him long enough to come up with a plan to get away. "Why Kit?"

Like a Cheshire cat that drank milk intended for someone else, he licked his lips, and she had to physically rein in the full-body shudder it evoked. "What is it that they say about keeping your friends close and your enemies closer?"

"So the whole time, your relationship was just a ploy? You were never in love with her?"

"I'm running a business, Heather, and if Kit had figured out what was going on, then she would have blown everything. Keeping her close was the easiest way to know how much the D.A.'s office knew."

"What did she figure out that cost her her life?"

Clay shrugged, running his hand through his hair. "Enough."

"That you were using PNW choppers to carry drugs across state lines?"

"Maybe. But it doesn't really matter. She wasn't worth the hassle anymore."

Heather fought the rush of tears that burned her eyes at the way he so flippantly dismissed the life of someone she loved so dearly. "So just like that, you sabotaged the helicopter to get rid of her?"

"Of course not. I don't know the first thing about helicopters. I have people for that."

"Geoff? Or maybe Newt?"

He lifted one shoulder. "Newt doesn't have the stomach for the details. He was happy to carry my merchandise, but the minute I suggested he might need to lose one of his precious birds, he wilted like a lily. Geoff, on the other hand, was more than happy to meet the chopper when it stopped to refuel." He lifted two fingers to form scissors. "Snip, snip."

Heather's stomach rolled. "What about the pilot? He must have known about the drugs or he wouldn't have stopped to pick them up."

"I couldn't have him thinking anything was different about that flight, could I?" He spoke to her as though she were a very small child with no reasoning skills. "Of course he picked up a package when he stopped."

"But you wasted those drugs."

Another shrug, as though he was bored with the conversation. "A small price for getting rid of Kit and whatever she had discovered."

"But then…if you didn't know what Kit knew, why did you try to have me killed at the hospital?" Her voice shook, the tenuous hold on her emotions slipping with each passing second as anger began to blot out her fear.

"Don't act like a fool, Heather." He shook his head, his gelled hair barely moving. "I knew perfectly well that you wouldn't let your sister's case rest like you should. You have no idea how much time I had to spend listening to her talk about how close you were and how she would do anything for you, blah, blah, blah." He sounded like he wanted to hurl, but in the growing shadows she couldn't see his face any longer.

"You were supposed to be collateral damage in the

crash, but after you didn't die from the overdose and the break-in, I thought Geoff's bomb on your SUV would take care of the situation. But clearly if I want this handled right, I'll have to do it myself."

The hand, which must have been exhausted from holding the gun for so long, wavered slightly and Heather made a careful move to the side.

"I assume that it was Geoff who broke into my house and vandalized it as well?" He barely nodded before she continued. "And your attack was staged to throw us off your trail?" She didn't even need his answer to that.

His sigh indicated he was through with the long-suffering interview. "Enough questions."

"Wait!" She held out one palm toward him, looking around frantically for any sign of help.

"It's too late. You're done."

As if in slow motion, his finger began to constrict around the trigger.

Heart pounding so loudly that it blocked out every other sound, she gasped to fill her lungs. But it was all to no avail.

Suddenly a voice that she'd know anywhere, called out across the rolling grass. "Hey! Hold it right there, Kramer! Don't move!" Jeremy barreled toward Heather and Clay, his arms outstretched, pointing his gun at Clay, shoulders rising and falling with rapid breaths. His quick steps barely favored the injury she'd noticed the day before.

Clay hardly glanced at the other man out of the corner of his eye, a smug expression planted across his features. But Heather couldn't keep her heart from tripling in speed, each thud physically painful in the tightness of her chest. She tried to snatch a deep breath, but her muscles were like stone.

When Jeremy was still fifty feet from them, Clay spun, pointing the gun at Jeremy. The report echoed among the trees, ringing in Heather's ears so that she couldn't even hear her own scream as Jeremy crumbled to the ground.

"You vile—" Her words ended before she really knew what she was saying. Instead, she picked up one of her crutches and swung it at him like a baseball bat.

She felt rather than heard the crunch of metal against his arm, and he fell to the ground in a heap as she took a second shot. The rubber of the under armrest connected with his temple, sending his face whipping away from her.

She stooped and snatched his gun from where it had fallen, resting her finger on the trigger and pointing it at his head.

He deserved it. For everything he'd done to Kit.

For everything he'd stolen from Heather.

He deserved to die.

The rage that shot through her veins and made her want to pull the trigger also stole her breath. She fought to fill her lungs, as the pain of Clay's betrayal ripped through her entire being.

Still, the gun didn't waver.

This was for Kit.

Revenge.

The air that she had worked so hard to inhale, left in a whoosh as the truth crashed around her. Jeremy had been right. She hadn't been looking for justice. She'd been looking for vengeance.

Oh, how she wanted this horrible man to suffer as she had, to lose the thing most important to him, his own life. How easy it would be to dispatch him right there.

Her finger shook on the trigger, but she couldn't squeeze it. Couldn't look at the unconscious man and steal his life as surely as he'd taken Kit from her.

Regardless of what he deserved, in the end sending off a single shot would only rob her of something she could never gain again.

Her peace of mind.

With the toe of her shoe, she rolled him over and leaned over to cuff him.

Then stealing herself for the worst possible situation, she hurried in the direction where Jeremy had fallen. Almost immediately she saw his limp form, then she was falling beside him and rolling him onto his back.

He groaned, opening one eye filled with pain. "I think—I think he shot me."

Heather chuckled through tears she hadn't even noticed until they streamed down her face. "Where does it hurt?"

"My leg." The crimson stain on his left pant leg steadily grew as blood seeped from the bullet wound.

"Hang in there. I'm calling 9-1-1 right now," she said as she dialed with one hand and cupped his cheek with the other.

He grimaced and closed both eyes. "Did you shoot him?"

She opened her mouth to answer, but he had passed out again.

The lawn was perfect, every blade of grass equal length, granite headstones glistening in the morning sun. As Heather stopped to catch her breath and give her knee a moment to stop shaking, she squinted up into the brilliant sky.

It seemed out of place, like the clouds should have

covered the sun. If ever there was a day for dreary, overcast skies, this was it.

But she had to make this walk, as though in a spotlight.

Picking her foot up again, she took a hesitant step toward the next row of markers.

When she spotted the stone she was looking for, just where her mom had said it would be, a band around her heart squeezed as though it would never loosen. But the words and dates were clear, even polished.

Katherine Anne Sloan
August 11, 1980—February 19, 2011

Had it really been nearly three weeks?
It felt like a lifetime had passed since the crash.
It felt like yesterday.

Heather lifted the bouquet of wildflowers to her nose one last time before bending awkwardly to set them in the little bucket attached to the stone.

"Hey, sis," she whispered into the breeze, just needing to share the pain in her heart. "I miss you. A lot." She swallowed and wiped away a tear from each eye, but for the first time not trying to stem the flow.

"A lot's happened, but I guess you know that." A hiccup caught her off guard, and brought an unexpected smile to her lips. "You always had the loudest hiccups. But I guess you won't have to deal with them anymore, will you?"

The wind blew a piece of grass onto the marker, and she brushed it away with the toe of her shoe. "I love you, Kit, and…well, I hope that you'd have been proud of me."

"I'm sure she would have been."

The deep voice behind her made her jump, but she didn't have to turn around to know that Jeremy stood there. If she hadn't recognized his voice, she couldn't miss the way her heart pounded and stomach turned whenever he was near.

"How did you know I'd be here?"

"Process of elimination. You weren't at home, and Nate hadn't seen you today." He made a familiar metallic click as he moved closer, and she spun, immediately eyeing the black walking cast below the frayed leg of his jeans.

"Are you—I mean, what did the doctor say?"

After all the terrible things she'd said to him the last time they'd really spoken, she didn't know what to say. She'd been too afraid to face him at the hospital three nights before. There had been questions from the police and reports to give. And once the nurse had told her that "the handsome patient in room four" was going to be fine, Heather had turned into a chicken. Afraid he'd send her away. Afraid she wouldn't have the words to apologize, she'd hidden away for days.

Now she couldn't bear to look into his face, so she resigned to staring at the eighteen inches of his cast, from ankle to knee.

He shifted his weight, leaning onto his right crutch and keeping all of his weight off the injured leg.

"The bullet cracked my shinbone, but it's going to heal. I'll just be on desk duty for a while after my official medical leave ends." In his shadow, his head moved as though trying to look into her eyes, but she couldn't bring herself to really face him.

"I'm sorry that you were shot."

He snickered. "Me, too."

Her cheeks burned, but not from the heat of the sun. "I mean, I'm sorry that you were shot coming to rescue me."

His shadow shrugged. "I'm not."

At the note of mercy in his tone, she managed to lift her gaze, but only to where his hands rested on the foam grips. Strong, tan and capable of handling anything that came his way. And he'd only been injured because of her foolishness.

She opened her mouth but had no words, so silence covered them for what felt like hours.

Finally Jeremy spoke, his words soft. "Did you hear that Clay's been arraigned and his trial has been scheduled to start next month?"

She nodded, her hair falling in front of her face.

"He's hired Lee Cooper, the best defense attorney in the city."

"I heard."

He seemed to want her to continue, but she didn't know what to say.

"He could get off free and clear." He took a step toward her, cutting the distance between them in half. Then he laid his hand on her upper arm. "Why didn't you take him out when you had the chance?"

Of all her actions that terrible night, not taking that shot was the only one she didn't regret. But how could she explain it to the man who knew how dark her heart had been?

"I thought I wanted to. I thought he deserved it. And I was afraid to trust that God would take care of it." When she paused to inhale, he hooked his forefinger under her chin and tilted it up until her eyes locked on his. She couldn't rip her gaze away from the molten chocolate pools there. He nodded, encouraging her to continue.

"I guess I just realized that showing mercy to Clay released me from having to regret something I couldn't take back. It put the responsibility for justice right back where it should have always been, and I feel freer now, like that weight I was carrying is gone."

"I'm proud of you, Heather."

She ripped her chin from where it still rested on his finger, breaking eye contact and fighting the tears that threatened once again. "Don't be. I was so mean, and I hurt you. And I was selfish and stupid. And I don't deserve for you to say anything like that to me."

The shadow Jeremy shook his head again, and when he spoke, his lips were just inches from her ear, sending shivers exploding down her spine. "I *am* proud of you. Clay wasn't going to give you the same mercy that you showed him. And as for what you said, you were right."

"I was?" She held her breath waiting for his response.

"I've been holding on to Reena's death like a badge, like a reminder that I don't deserve love if I can't promise protection in return. But I forgot that it's not up to me to protect those I love." He squeezed her arm, sending bolts of electricity to her fingertips. "Thank you for reminding me that God is our protector."

Fighting the desire to keep her eyes averted, Heather forced her gaze back to Jeremy's face. She couldn't read his emotions, but she had to know. "Do you still love Reena?"

A tiny smile lifted the corner of his lips. "I'll always remember her, but I've let her go. Mostly, I think, because I've recently realized that I can love someone else."

"You ca-an?" She didn't even worry about her voice cracking as her heart nearly stopped. She licked her lips, longing to hear the words that had been on her heart, too.

"Don't sound so shocked." With a wicked grin he leaned in and whispered against her lips. "I love you, Heather Sloan."

She couldn't even respond before she closed the distance, kissing him with all the emotion she'd been harboring since the crash. Like security and faithfulness, he surrounded her, wrapping an arm around her waist and tugging her against him.

He felt like comfort after a nightmare, a safe harbor after a terrible storm. Like the man she would love forever.

She shuffled even closer to him, until her knee brace connected with his cast.

They both laughed but didn't pull away.

"So what are we going to do now?" He brushed her hair behind her ear, leaving a hand on the side of her neck.

"Well, we have some time to figure it out." He quirked an eyebrow and she smiled. "I'm on disciplinary probation. Until my knee heals completely. Nate said it was his only chance to get me to rest enough to actually recover."

Jeremy chuckled and leaned in for another quick kiss.

When he pulled back, Heather looked over her shoulder, a heaviness in her heart breaking the levity. "I wish Kit could have known you better."

"I wish I could have known her. She sounds like a pretty amazing woman." He squeezed her hand. "A lot like her sister."

"I do love you, Jeremy Latham."

"Good." His grin returned. "I was getting worried when you didn't say it back."

She swatted his arm playfully as they strolled down the row, toward a future filled with love and laughter.

* * * * *

Dear Reader,

Like most kids, my sister and I didn't always get along as we were growing up. But during one pivotal semester in college, we lived together, studied together and truly discovered what it meant to be friends. Now we live almost 2,000 miles apart, but by the grace of God that bond has remained, growing stronger over the years so that I can truthfully call her my best friend.

Like my sister and me, Heather and Kit shared a special bond. When it was broken, Heather became so consumed with avenging Kit's death that she stopped listening to God's direction for her life, stopped trusting God's justice would prevail. Of course, Jeremy struggled with a similar problem—carrying guilt over something that ultimately was never in his control.

I pray that after reading Heather and Jeremy's story, you'll be encouraged and reminded that God is always in control. We won't always understand His plan this side of heaven, but we can trust in who God is. He has proven Himself faithful, and He is a just God, whose mercies are new every morning.

Thank you for spending time with us. I'd love to hear from you and what you thought of this book. You can e-mail me at liz@lizjohnsonbooks.com or visit my website at www.lizjohnsonbooks.com. Thanks again for joining me on this adventure. I hope we have many more to come.

Liz Johnson

QUESTIONS FOR DISCUSSION

1. What was your favorite part of the book?

2. Who was your favorite character? What made you relate to him/her?

3. Heather and Kit shared a special bond as sisters. Do you have a sibling with whom you are very close? What makes your relationship special?

4. What differences do you generally see between relationships with brothers and sisters?

5. Heather misses out on the opportunity to go to Kit's funeral. How do you think that affects Heather's drive to find the man responsible for Kit's death?

6. After the crash, Heather's friend Nora offers to help her, but Heather asks her not to come by. Why do you think it is often so difficult for women to accept help, even when they're really in need?

7. Heather is so consumed with avenging Kit's death that her prayers feel like they're just bouncing off the ceiling. Have you ever gotten to a point where you felt your prayers were useless? How did you get through that time?

8. Jeremy's been living with the guilt over losing Reena for a long time. Is there something in your life that you regret and have been carrying with you? What do you need to do to let it go?

9. When Jeremy is finally ready to talk to someone about Reena, he chooses his friend Tony. What qualities in their friendship do you think allow Jeremy to be so honest?

10. What friends have you had that you knew you could be honest with? Did they share any characteristics with Tony?

11. Heather and Jeremy have a fight when Heather says that she's going to put herself out as bait for the killer. She feels desperate, as though this is her only option to solve the case. What would you do if you were in that position? Would you put your own life on the line?

12. Most of us will never know the loss combined with the extreme fear that Heather and Jeremy face in the book. This makes them both doubt God's plans. What have you been through that has made you doubt God? How did God prove Himself in your life?

Love Inspired®
SUSPENSE

TITLES AVAILABLE NEXT MONTH

Available April 12, 2011

MURDER AT GRANITE FALLS
Big Sky Secrets
Roxanne Rustand

TRAIL OF LIES
Texas Ranger Justice
Margaret Daley

POINT BLANK PROTECTOR
Emerald Coast 911
Stephanie Newton

HOUSE OF SECRETS
Ramona Richards

LISCNM0311

REQUEST YOUR FREE BOOKS!

2 FREE RIVETING INSPIRATIONAL NOVELS
PLUS 2 FREE MYSTERY GIFTS

YES! Please send me 2 FREE Love Inspired® Suspense novels and my 2 FREE mystery gifts (gifts are worth about $10). After receiving them, if I don't wish to receive any more books, I can return the shipping statement marked "cancel". If I don't cancel, I will receive 4 brand-new novels every month and be billed just $4.24 per book in the U.S. or $4.74 per book in Canada. That's a saving of at least 23% off the cover price. It's quite a bargain! Shipping and handling is just 50¢ per book in the U.S. and 75¢ per book in Canada.* I understand that accepting the 2 free books and gifts places me under no obligation to buy anything. I can always return a shipment and cancel at any time. Even if I never buy another book, the two free books and gifts are mine to keep forever.

123/323 IDN FDCT

Name	(PLEASE PRINT)	
Address		Apt. #
City	State/Prov.	Zip/Postal Code

Signature (if under 18, a parent or guardian must sign)

Mail to the **Reader Service:**
IN U.S.A.: P.O. Box 1867, Buffalo, NY 14240-1867
IN CANADA: P.O. Box 609, Fort Erie, Ontario L2A 5X3

Not valid for current subscribers to Love Inspired Suspense books.

**Are you a subscriber to Love Inspired Suspense
and want to receive the larger-print edition?
Call 1-800-873-8635 or visit www.ReaderService.com.**

* Terms and prices subject to change without notice. Prices do not include applicable taxes. Sales tax applicable in N.Y. Canadian residents will be charged applicable taxes. Offer not valid in Quebec. This offer is limited to one order per household. All orders subject to credit approval. Credit or debit balances in a customer's account(s) may be offset by any other outstanding balance owed by or to the customer. Please allow 4 to 6 weeks for delivery. Offer available while quantities last.

Your Privacy—The Reader Service is committed to protecting your privacy. Our Privacy Policy is available online at www.ReaderService.com or upon request from the Reader Service.

We make a portion of our mailing list available to reputable third parties that offer products we believe may interest you. If you prefer that we not exchange your name with third parties, or if you wish to clarify or modify your communication preferences, please visit us at www.ReaderService.com/consumerchoice or write to us at Reader Service Preference Service, P.O. Box 9062, Buffalo, NY 14269. Include your complete name and address.

LISUS11